# THE PLAINS OF L          O

# THE PLAINS OF LARAMIE

## A WESTERN TRIO

## LAURAN PAINE

**FIVE STAR**

*An imprint of Thomson Gale, a part of The Thomson Corporation*

Detroit • New York • San Francisco • New Haven, Conn. • Waterville, Maine • London

Set in 11 pt. Plantin.

**LIBRARY OF CONGRESS CATALOGING-IN-PUBLICATION DATA**

Paine, Lauran.
    The plains of Laramie : a western trio / by Lauran Paine. — 1st ed.
    p. cm.
    ISBN 1-59414-397-8 (hardcover : alk. paper) 1. Western stories. I. Title.
PS3566.A34P63 2006
813'.54—dc22                                                      2006018303

U.S. Hardcover:
ISBN 13:978-1-59414-397-7
ISBN 10:1-59414-397-8

First Edition. First Printing: October 2006.

Published in 2006 in conjunction with Golden West Literary Agency.

Printed in the United States of America on permanent paper
10 9 8 7 6 5 4 3 2 1

# CONTENTS

★ ★ ★ ★ ★

# Boothill's Ferryman

★ ★ ★ ★ ★

# I

A covey of prairie chickens darted frantically through the brush as Jack Masters threaded his way down off the slight bluff that overlooked the ferry landing. He heard their scared *croaks* as they tried to keep within distance of each other, as they lumbered through the underbrush, but his blue eyes were drinking in the raw beauty of the scene ahead, where the Modoc River swung in a wide, graceful arc through the flat prairie. The river was a clean, steely color under the late fall sunshine. Jack let his gaze wander from the great sweep of land on the far side of the river to the squatty adobe house that nestled next to the sloping riverbank, where a pair of flat-bottomed ferries hugged the bank drowsily, their weathered sides and decks rippling gently under the force of the current.

Masters felt the hint of autumn in the air. It was warm but there was a coolness, too, that meant winter wasn't far off. He dismounted slowly and tied his horse to a patched hitch rack near the house. An odor of water and marsh mud came to him. He methodically loosened the latigo a little and gave the cinch a mild tug that left it hanging below his horse's stomach.

Jack Masters wasn't a talkative man. A sheriff of many years' standing, he had come to look on people and life in general as a routine that required a little steering, a little regulating now and then, but not a lot of unnecessary vocal labor. He turned away from the hitch rack, gave an unconscious tug at his sagging gun belt, and surveyed the familiar scene with thoughtful, quiet eyes.

Cobb's Ferry was an old place; no one remembered who the first owner and founder had been. Probably some enterprising Yankee emigrant with an eye to a comfortable living—and possibly trail-weary, too—had built some barges and worked up the business that had, down through the years, become a mainstay of life and an essential service to the territory. There wasn't a man, woman, or child who didn't cross the Modoc at Cobb's Ferry at least a dozen times a year. It was the shortest and best route between the hamlet of Mendocino and the comparative metropolis of Rawlins, whence came the supplies for the little cow town.

Jack's somber gaze went to the ancient adobe house. Since the new owner—a blustering, mean-visaged man by the name of Tolliver—had bought out the aged prior owner, a little friction had come up. In the first place, Tolliver had trebled the crossing rates, which, naturally, didn't go over very well with the local folks in Mendocino. Then, too, Tolliver, a heavy drinker, was given to high-handed ways and sly remarks. Jack had heard all of these things, and he knew that the temper of the cowmen and their families was dangerously near the eruption point. For that reason and no other, he had ridden down to the ferry to have a talk with Link Tolliver. Sheriff Masters was a firm believer in quenching trouble before it flared up, if possible. He sauntered over toward the house, his high-heeled boots leaving small, disconnected imprints in the dry path; his spurs rang out softly, musically in the hushed atmosphere.

A liver-colored hound, gaunt and red-eyed, growled ominously as Jack stepped up onto the little slab gallery someone had built many years before to shade the square front of the house from summer's everlasting glare in the treeless clearing. He looked appraisingly at the hound, saw the sleepy, annoyed look in its eyes, and walked on up to the half closed door and banged on it with his gloved fist. There was a squeaking, groaning sound from within and a thick, heavy-bellied man in a red undershirt, with mud-colored eyes and a three days' growth of graying whiskers, loomed up in the doorway.

Link Tolliver was every bit as tall as Sheriff Masters, even in his bare feet. He was paunchy and sagging, though, where Jack was straight and lean. He nodded owlishly at the sheriff and stood impassively barring the doorway.

Jack forced a smile with an effort. "Howdy, Link. Was ridin' by an' thought I'd stop in an' have a little talk with you."

"Yeah?" The big, heavy-jowled face was wary. Tolliver made no move to ask the sheriff in. "What about?"

Jack shrugged, backed up a little, and sat on the railing that went around the small gallery. He thumbed his black Stetson to the back of his head. There was mild annoyance in his eyes at the lack of cow-country hospitality in the gross man before him. Without any preliminary he opened up. "There's talk up in town, Link. Some of the folks seem a little irked at your new prices fer crossin' the river, an' some of the boys sort o' resent your remarks when they've got their women an' kids along."

Tolliver shifted a little on his splayed feet, his blank eyes balefully on the lawman. "Well, s'long as it's my ferry, I kin charge what I damned well please. Ain't no law governin' that . . . yet. An' if folks don't like the things I say . . . why, then, I reckon they don't have to come here, do they?"

Masters flushed a little and looked away, letting his glance slide over the drowsing hound so that Tolliver wouldn't see the cloudy look in his eyes. "No, I don't reckon folks *have* to cross here, Link." He got off the railing and started for the edge of the porch. "Only I thought I'd drop by an' let you know that there's some bad blood buildin' up. If I were you, I'd sort o' go a little easy. These cowmen around Mendocino haven't been too many years away from gun law, you know, an' maybe someone of 'em'll get hostile." The lean, capable shoulders rose and fell meaningfully. "Somebody might get hurt, an' I'd like to see that avoided, if it's possible."

Tolliver's laugh came out to Jack where he stopped on the path leading to his horse at the hitch rack. "Thanks, Sheriff. Link Tolliver's seen his share o' trouble, I allow, an' I ain't seen anyone hereabouts that could teach him much. Let 'em come, Sheriff. They'll get the damnedest surprise o' their cow-stealin' lives!"

Masters clamped his jaw shut as a hot reply came lunging up from inside. He nodded curtly and walked back to his horse, tightened the cinch, swung aboard, and reined back up the trail toward Mendocino, the town that lay a couple of miles beyond the little swale that hid the view of the Modoc from its sight.

In Mendocino, the tag end of a gentle summer had come to a close and the cowmen were left with only one task left undone. They had grassed-out fat cattle to peddle, the hay was up, and the firewood was in. The roundups were winding up their arduous labors, and the cowmen were beginning to drift into town to talk in the shade of the old sycamores, where a light carpet of dead leaves betokened winter. Prices, possible outlets, and the condition of critters were the standard norms of daily conversation. Jack Masters watched the repetitive cycle that year, as he had every year since he had been a young cowboy—newly come to the high uplands of the Mendocino country to put down roots of his own.

He was in the Goldstrike Saloon, one of Mendocino's two such establishments, when Wes Flourney, his young, effervescent deputy, came bouncing in. Masters smiled at the younger man.

"Say, Jack, d'ya hear about Ned Prouty?"

Jack thought of short, waspish Ned—grizzled and hard as

flint, but fair and honest, one of the few remaining pioneer cow-men of the Mendocino. He shook his head slightly, gazing indif-ferently out over the buzzing groups of cattlemen standing and sitting around the saloon, busy with talk of cows and beef. He was almost beyond the reach of Wes's voice, and the words for a second didn't penetrate, but, when they did, Sheriff Masters swung abruptly around, the tolerant smile gone from his lean, tanned face.

"What'd you say, Wes?"

"Ol' Ned an' that Tolliver *hombre,* over at the ferry, tangled this mornin'. Tolliver shot him. He's over at his ranch now an' his two boys swear they're goin' to kill Tolliver."

Jack paid for his lukewarm beer, faced around again, and frowned. "Wes, you keep an eye on things in town. I'm goin' out to the Pothook." Wes nodded speculatively.

The Pothook was one of the historic cow outfits of the Men-docino country. When Jack rode up to the sprawling old house, he noted the solemn, hard eyes of the riders hanging around the bunkhouse and the barn. He nodded as he rode by, up to the hitch rail, and went on to the house on foot. A square-jawed, short, and muscular young man met him with a harsh smile. "Reckon you want to see Pa?"

"That's right, Bud. How is he?"

The shorter man shrugged coldly. "About as good as any old fella shot in the back can be, I reckon."

"Shot in the back?"

The young man, one of Ned Prouty's sons, nodded and beckoned the sheriff inside. "Come on, Jack, he can talk to you all right." They were almost to the doorway of the old man's bedchamber when another man, dark and square-jawed and a little taller than Bud Prouty, came out with a savage expression on his swarthy features. Jack nodded to him. Cal Prouty was one of the best cowboys in the Mendocino country. He glared at Jack for a long moment, then pushed past without a word. Bud flushed a little but made no excuse for his brother. Jack shrugged and entered the sick room.

Ned Prouty was deathly pale but his faded gray eyes were like twin coals under the bushy eyebrows. "Howdy, Jack. Set yourself." Masters sat, dropped his hat to the floor beside his chair, and looked questioningly at the little hump of flesh under the white blankets and quilts.

Prouty nodded slightly. "Asked the varmint to keep that danged hound o' his from chasin' Pothook cows. He's hell on 'em, Jack, calves, too." The thin old shoulders rose and fell. "He said to keep my cows away from his place, an' I told him that this was a free range country where a man's gotta fence 'em out if he don't want 'em on his land. Well, he got sore, I reckon. Anyway, he started talkin' rough. I called him. He didn't say nothin', just stood there on his porch an' glared at me. He wasn't armed . . . or, at least I didn't see no gun. I told him to keep the damned dawg offen my cows or I'd kill it. Went back to get on my horse an' damned if he didn't pot me as I was ridin' away. I got damned near home afore I fell off. The boys found me an' brung me in. That's all there is to it, Jack . . . couple of words an' a shot in the back." He nodded bird-like, matter-of-factly, and waited for Jack to speak.

"How's the wound, Ned?"

"Doc Sunday says I'll make it all right. Close, he says, but not fatal."

"How soon'll you be up an' around, Ned?"

"Week mebbe. Ten days. Why?"

Jack got up, put his hat on absently, and looked out the window at the waving, dry grass on the range beyond the house. "Well, I'll go down an' arrest him for attempted murder, Ned. I'll have to hold him until you can testify against him, so let me know as soon's you get up, and come in, will you?"

"Bet your life, Jack."

# II

The sun was well past the meridian when Jack rode down the dusty little trail, age-old and bare, that led down to Cobb's Ferry. This time his face was a mask of wariness and resolution. Once having tried to avoid trouble he knew was coming, Sheriff Jack Masters felt no reluctance at all about ruthlessly stamping it out after his warning had been ignored. He rode directly up to the adobe house without dismounting, leaned over in the saddle, and called out for Tolliver to come out.

There was an unreal silence around the old house and Masters sensed a tension before the door opened slowly and a heavily muscled young man came out. He wore a gun tied down in its worn, shiny holster on his right leg. He didn't say anything right away, looking Jack over with a challenging insolence. "Who you want?"

"Link Tolliver."

"He ain't here."

"Where is he?"

"Don't know."

Jack tossed a look past the house to the decayed old corral of tree trunks, round and massive but rotting away with age. There were three strange horses in there with fresh sweat on them and three saddles lay in the dust just outside, but Tolliver's huge gray mare wasn't in sight. He looked around the house and saw that the hound was gone, too. Apparently the cold-eyed young man was telling the truth.

He brought his gaze back to the baleful, sullen face. "What's your name, *hombre?*" There was no mistaking the earnestness in the voice and the round, unwashed countenance reddened a little.

"Name's Tolliver. Ben Tolliver. Though I don't see as it's ary o' your bizness, lawman."

Masters regarded the other with a somber glance as he took up the slack in his reins. "Ben, when Link gets back, tell him I'm lookin' for him an' I'll be back in the mornin'." He was turning his horse when he heard a shuffling sound on the slab porch and looked back. Two more men were standing beside Ben. He took a long look at them and felt misgivings. Each was as hard-looking as Ben, with tied-down guns, ferret-like faces, and malevolent, cold eyes. He rode back down the trail to Mendocino, aware that three pair of hostile eyes followed him in silence.

Wes Flourney walked into the sheriff's combination jail and office with the first streaks of the new day. He nodded at Jack, who sat behind his desk with a sober, worried look on his face. "It ain't that bad, is it, Sheriff?"

"What?"

The deputy shrugged. "Whatever you're thinkin' about. Man, your face looks like the last rose of summer."

"Just thinkin', Wes. I rode down to get Link Tolliver last evenin', an' he wasn't there. But three more Tollivers were, an' they aren't attractive specimens, either." He scratched his head and yanked his gracefully curved Stetson lower on his head. "Wes, can you go out an' sort o' keep those Prouty boys from doin' anythin' rash, like ridin' down to Tolliver's for the balance o' the day?"

"I can sure try, Jack. Maybe their dad'll help by tellin' 'em to stay on the Pothook."

"Yeah, I reckon he might at that. Well, ride on over there an' keep those fire-eaters off Tolliver for today. After that, I won't care. I'll have the bushwhacker in jail, where I can keep an eye on him, an' those boys won't be gettin' into serious trouble by tryin' to do him in."

"*Seguro, jefe,* I'll do my damnedest. S'long." Wes swung through the door to the musical accompaniment of his tinkling spurs with their huge Chihuahua rowels. "Keep an eye on them Tollivers. If there's three more of 'em now, you'd better step light."

Masters nodded without answering and sat for another five minutes or so after young Flourney had gone. When he emerged from his office, and tightened the cinch on his horse at the hitch rack, four graying cowmen came up beside him. He turned to face them. "Howdy, gents. Out kind of early, aren't you?"

The spokesman for the quartet nodded brusquely. "We're on our way to havin' a showdown with that there coyote who owns Cobb's Ferry now."

Jack shook his head peremptorily. "You boys stick to the cow business an' let me handle Tolliver."

"Not by a damned sight, Jack. He's got a necktie party comin' up, an' the decent folk hereabouts figger he's due to get it?"

Masters's eyes were grave and unblinking as he surveyed the red-faced cowmen. "You fellers go down there an' there'll be shootin'. Link Tolliver's got some kinsmen down there with him, an' they look like pretty fair gunmen to me." He swung up on his horse and looked down with a frown at the ranchers. "Anyway, this is my job. I don't come out to your ranches an' butt in an' I don't want you fellas buttin' into my lawing business. Stay away from the ferry, boys, or I'll toss the whole damned bunch of you in the *calabozo.*"

The big man snorted violently and glared at the sheriff. Masters fixed him with a cold, menacing stare and his voice, always slow and soft, was very quiet when next he spoke. "I mean it, boys. Stay away from Tolliver's place." The cowmen watched him ride out of Mendocino without saying a word. Somebody suggested getting an early morning eye-opener and they adjourned sullenly to the Goldstrike.

Link Tolliver was waiting for him. Jack could see him standing in the clearing before the adobe hut as he jogged down the path toward the river. Jack's eyes were slitted and wary without a nod or a word as he rode up. Link was armed this time; a battered old six-gun was strapped low on his thigh with a thong around the massive leg. A Winchester carbine was leaning lazily against his arm.

"Get your horse, Link!"

Link's muddy eyes were hard and staring. "What fer, lawman?"

Jack didn't relax; he sensed a stall. "Rope it, Link. You know damned well what for. Get your horse an' damned fast!"

"Not by a damned sight! Ain't no lawman goin' to come a-ridin' onto my propitty an' commence orderin' me around."

Masters relaxed his arm, and his mouth was a bloodless line over wolfish teeth. "You're comin' to Mendocino with me *on* a horse or across one. Shootin' Ned Prouty in the back is attempted murder hereabouts. You're goin' to answer for it. Now either get your horse or fill your hand."

Tolliver's lined, bewhiskered face split in a sardonic smile. "Look behind you, Sheriff. They's three *hombres* that done slipped up on you, an' a word from me'll send you to hell in a hand basket." The evil smile widened as Jack held Link Tolliver with his deadly stare. Suddenly Tolliver's face lost the smile and his eyes bugged a little. He was staring into the maw of a cocked six-shooter in the sheriff's hand. He hadn't seen the hand dip toward the holster at all; he licked his lips with a furtive tongue.

"Drop that rifle, Link." Hesitatingly the big man relaxed his hold and the .30-30 plopped into the dust. "Now, Link, tell your boys to come around in front of me or I'll squeeze this trigger." Link shifted his eyes from beyond the lawman's horse, then swung his eyes back again. Masters's fingers tightened on the trigger. His voice was little more than a whisper. "Link, whether I'm shot or not, I can't miss you at this distance, an' you know it . . . even dyin' I can kill you. Now shuck your pistol an' call 'em off."

Tolliver's beaten expression was redolent with hatred. He called to his kinsmen, explained the situation, and tossed his six-gun to the ground. The three Tollivers came around in front of Jack with enraged and baffled faces.

Without taking his eyes off Link, Masters said: "One of you go saddle Link's horse an' bring it around. The other two of you stay here." The youngest of the three—the one called Ben—slouched off toward the old corral with a snarled oath. Masters wanted to make the others disarm, but hesitated to push his luck too far. The four of them waited in dry-eyed tension until Ben brought back Tolliver's horse.

"Get aboard, Link." The sheriff untied his lariat from the swells with his left hand and flipped the noose to Link. "Over your head, around the neck." He smiled grimly at Link's flushed, humiliated look. "Now come up close, so's you're between me an' your kinsmen."

Link was getting redder every second, but he complied.

Masters waved his cocked .45 at the men afoot. "Toss your guns as far out into the river as you can, boys. One false move an' Link's a goner."

The men complied profanely and Jack Masters rode back toward Mendocino with Link behind him, protecting his back. The lariat rope around Link's throat was his sturdy assurance of seeing another sunset.

Wes Flourney checked into the sheriff's office when he came

back to Mendocino and saw the lamplight coming out of the barred window. He looked owlishly at Link Tolliver in his cell, went back in to the front office, and sighed. "*Phew!* That *hombre* looks more like a bushwhacker than a bushwhacker does." He rolled a cigarette with a weary gesture. "Say, d'ya ever try to keep an eye on two wildcats at the same time? *¡Hijo de puta!* I have today. Even after old Ned asked 'em to stick around, they was like a pair of fledgling magpies, sore at the world, mad at me fer hangin' around, an' sore at the old man, too, fer not lettin' 'em go over to Cobb's Ferry."

Masters laughed and got up, reaching for his hat where it dangled precariously from one tip of a four-point hatrack. "Well, it's all over now, Wes. Link'll stay here until Ned can get up and come in to prefer charges, then we'll have a trial, an' maybe Link'll draw a few years." He shrugged toward the door after blowing out the lamp. "Mendocino'll be peaceable again now . . . for a while, anyway."

Deputy Flourney shrugged out behind his employer and flicked the cigarette into a nearby rain barrel, full of greenish water. "It'll be a relief, by damn, not to have that nursemaid role any longer. G'night, Jack."

The sheriff was heading across the dusty road toward his rooms in the Mendocino Hotel above the Goldstrike Saloon when he answered with a friendly little nod: *"Buenas noches."*

With the first cold bitterness of predawn Jack Masters sat upright. Wes Flourney, dressed but disheveled, was bending over him, shaking him frantically "Wake up, Jack, dammit man, wake up."

"All right, you idiot, don't tear my arm off. Just what in hell's wrong with you? Lose your way home an' hang one on in the Goldstrike?"

"Jack"—Flourney's voice was high-keyed with excitement—

"the gather that was bein' held below the Pothook, in that box cañon the cowmen use to hold their critters before they drive 'em to the railroad over at Rawlins, was rustled clean as a hound's tooth last night."

Masters blinked his eyes owlishly at Wes. "How'd ya find out?"

Wes snorted loudly. "*Compadre,* there's just about every damned cowman this side o' New Mexico downstairs in the Goldstrike right now, screamin' their heads off. They want their cattle back, but more'n that they want someone's blood."

Masters swung out of his bed and dressed silently. The fall drive had been in the making for quite a few days now and finally each ranch had shoved its allocated critters into the gather preparatory to the communal drive to Rawlins. It was an annual affair, and Jack knew how the ranchers would feel. He also knew that there would be blood on the moon if their suspicions were ever fixed on specific individuals. He yawned prodigiously, yanked his Stetson low over his forehead, and cast a wistful glance at the rumpled, warm bed before following Wes downstairs.

Pandemonium was in full swing in the saloon. Most of the ranchers had come directly from their beds and showed it. They may have lacked some of the lesser necessities of sartorial equipment, but none of them had forgotten guns. Rifles were in evidence everywhere, across laps, leaning against chairs, under arms, and on the bar top, while the conventional six-gun was prominent on every leg. When Masters entered the room with his deputy, the furor swelled into a demanding, snarling tirade that roared and rumbled like a major waterfall of hoarse anger.

Jack shook his head slowly and held up his hand. "Dammit, one at a time, boys. Now, then, when do you figger it happened?"

Cal Prouty and his brother were sitting at a vacated poker

table. He frowned darkly. "No tellin', Jack . . . sometime last night is about all we know. The night hawk was knocked over the head. He's over at Everhart's place, still unconscious. The relief guards found him and set up the alarm. We tried trackin' 'em, but, when they got to the river, we had to drop it. Too dark." He got up suddenly and draped his stubby carbine over his arm. "It's light enough now, though. Come on, we'll show you where we last seen the sign."

# III

The night was begrudgingly giving way before the advance of the new day. Stars were flickering out, one by one, and the cold air was bracing in a man's lungs. There were at least a dozen in the bitter-faced clutch of cowmen that picked up the trail of the rustled cattle a mile this side of the Modoc. The trail was about eighty feet wide and easily discernible by the churned-up, blotched earth. Now and then the men found a horse hoof imprint. None of the hoof marks found, however, was made by a shod horse; apparently all of the rustlers rode barefoot horses. The trail went over the flat land in a straight line for the river-bank. Brush—waist high—was crushed to rubble in the dust. The men rode down a gentle slope and stopped at the river-bank. Several of them looked at Masters. He stared at the cold, uninviting water and made a wry face.

"Let's go to the ferry an' cross over there. Won't be wastin' much time, an' there's likely to be a lot of ridin' yet to come that none of us'll want to do wringin' wet."

The ranchers were of a like mind and rode the spongy river-bank downstream until they came to the still buildings of Cobb's Ferry. The noise of many horsemen was clear and sinister in the cold morning. Someone peeked out of the cabin, and Bud Prouty rode in close with his swarthy brother beside him.

"Come on out of there an' get that ferry unhitched. We want to get across that river."

There was no answer, and Masters, sensing the antagonism in the Prouty boys, kneed his horse up close to them. "Probably no one's in there."

The taller Prouty boy swore and dismounted. "Yes there is. We seen the door open a crack." He was up to the door when he finished speaking. Jerking his .45, he lunged out and swung a violent kick at the door. It flew inward with a *crash* and a jagged, fierce tongue of flame spewed out of the interior. Prouty folded up in the middle like a jackknife, squeezing off one shot as he went down. A terrible scream of rage came from Bud Prouty as he flung off his horse and tore inside the adobe house, gun belching death with livid splotches of flame that didn't quite drown out the animal cries that came in a virulent stream from his mouth.

Jack led the posse men who stormed up, red-eyed and lusting for blood. It was over as quickly as it had started. Bud Prouty came out of the house, ashen-faced and numb. He holstered his gun and knelt by his brother.

Jack Masters put a strong, gentle hand on his shoulder and the boy raised his eyes in disbelief. "Through the heart, Bud."

Someone was cursing as he dragged a limp body out of the adobe. Jack arose and went over to look at it. He nodded to the crowd of grim men. "It's one of the hardcase Tollivers that wasn't goin' to let me arrest Link yesterday."

One old rancher, who seemed rather exultant, kicked the body with a pointed-toed boot. His spur tinkled a knell in the quiet. "Well, he's one o' the scum that won't play hardcase no more. Four slugs in his mangy carcass. The last one right atween the eyes." He spat contemptuously on the warped planks beside the body and turned away.

The ranchers loaded themselves and their horses on the larger of the two wormy-hulled ferryboats and pulled silently for the other side while Bud Prouty had two of the younger hands strike out in a sad little procession for the Pothook with the burden of the dead cowboy athwart his led saddle horse.

"Let's go boys." Masters unloaded his horse, swung aboard, and headed back along the far bank for the spot where the stolen beef had been made to swim across. Once on the wide, rambling trail again, the cowmen swung into a mile-eating lope. Jack sent three of the younger cowmen, including Bud Prouty, on ahead to search for the herd. The sun was warming up the chilly air and the pristine light bathed the cold land in a blanket of fresh clearness. The trail was wider for a while, where the rustlers had allowed the critters to spread out over the grassy plain. Jack rode along silently. He alternated between scanning the broad distances and studying the unshod hoof marks. One of the outriders he had sent ahead came back driving two footsore steers before him.

"Brung these back to show you. They's eleven more in that skunk-brush thicket up yonder. Reckon they didn't want to bother with a few weary ones."

One rancher swore and pointed to the brand on the right rib of the critters. "Mine, by golly, Diamond E on 'em." He looked them over speculatively, noticed the slight shrink, and shrugged. "All right, leave 'em here. We'll pick 'em up on the way back."

The cavalcade moved on again. They rode for another hour before the distant sound of gunfire came riding down the still air to them.

Jack Masters held up a gloved fist and they came to an abrupt stop. "Two quick shots. Fan out boys, they must be up ahead."

The cowmen spurred into a run, brandishing their rifles in savage anticipation. Jack looked up and down the rough line of hard-riding cowmen that strung out over the plain and felt pride in their co-operation and courage. Suddenly, up ahead, he could see the milling herd of cattle, their red backs glistening under the sun, and then they were up to the herd. Bud Prouty rode a stiff-legged trot down to meet them. Jack set his horse as Bud came in close. "Ain't nobody here, Jack."

"The hell." Jack's eyes raked over the herd where it stood bunched up, heads down and weary. He scanned the surrounding plain in every direction and saw only a few straggling beeves but no riders. "D'ya see 'em, Bud?"

"Nary a sign. When we got up to the critters, they were standin' here like you see 'em. Wore out from bein' pushed half the night, but without no rustlers anywhere in sight." He wagged his head in perplexity. "Can't figger it at all."

Masters started in the saddle and ripped out an oath. He swung, wide-eyed, to Wes Flourney who was watching him with a puzzled look on his face. "A trap, boys, pure an' simple."

One of the ranchers was sliding his carbine back into the saddle boot as he spoke. "What in hell d'ya mean, a trap?" He rammed the butt down hard and swung his hand over the herd. "We got the critters back, ain't we?"

"Yeah," another cowman growled. "Not only got 'em back, but they're halfway to the shippin' pens at Rawlins. We might just as well take them the rest o' the way."

Jack was staring broodingly back over the trail they had just traveled. "Those men had no intention of stealin' your cattle. They just wanted to draw all of us away from Mendocino."

"What the hell for?"

"So's they could ride back an' bust Link Tolliver out of jail, that's what for."

Wes Flourney swore bitterly. "What a bunch of fools we are." His face mirrored complete disgust. "I'll bet they left that one *hombre* at Cobb's Ferry fer a spy, or somethin'. Maybe they even figgered he'd steer us after the herd, an' see that we took the right trail. After that he was supposed to join 'em, I'll bet."

"Yeah? Then why in hell did he shoot young Prouty?"

Wes was warming to his theory. "That's easy. When Prouty busted in on him, it scairt him. He figgered maybe somethin' had gone wrong an' we was a posse come after him. He fired because he was scairt and cornered, same as any rat would do."

Jack turned to the cowmen, picked out four of them to form his posse, and left the others to continue the cattle drive to Rawlins. They separated then, each group going its own way. Jack jogged back toward the ferry with his face sober and grim. It rankled a little to be outwitted by the Tolliver clan, but he dared not rush back pell-mell. The horses were tired enough as it was, what with the hard riding they had received in their search for the lost herd.

Back at the ferry the posse men loaded their horses for the return trip, pulled for the opposite shore, unloaded, and swung aboard in wary silence. They jogged, hard-eyed, past the adobe house and gazed dispassionately on the stiffening body still sprawled on the gray planking of the porch. Single file they navigated the bluff trail and swung into a lope for the last mile of the return trip to town.

Mendocino was in an uproar as Jack, Wes, and Bud Prouty at the head of the cowman posse rode up through town toward the livery barn. Grant Yates, the fat, florid president of the Mendocino State Bank came running out into the road to flag them down. His hands were shaking when he put them on the neck of Jack's sweaty horse.

"Good gawd, Sheriff! The bank, it's been robbed! We've lost the savings of half the people in Mendocino County!"

The complete cunning of the Tollivers burst in upon the sheriff and he swung down in silence, pushed the banker away, and led his horse into the livery stable.

Jack Masters was white-faced. Calamity far, far worse than a rustled herd of cattle was overwhelming him. The liveryman saw it on his ashen face and in his glowing eyes when he came up. "Ed, me an' the boys here need fresh horses. How about puttin' our rigs on fresh stock while we're findin' out the worst?"

The liveryman nodded quickly. "Sure, Jack, sure. Have 'em ready fer you soon as you want 'em." He wagged his head sympathetically. "Hell to pay, Jack. Mendocino's about cleaned out." He took Masters's reins and pointed toward the bank, next door to the Goldstrike Saloon. "They kilt a man in there." As Jack turned to his posse men, the liveryman yelled for his hostlers, and a furious bustling among the barn men and the drooping posse horses evidenced the liveryman's speedy labors.

Jack turned to Flourney, and motioned for the others to quiet down. "Lope over to the jail, Wes, an' see if Link's still there. Meet me at the bank." He was walking away as he spoke. Flourney nodded quickly and started for the jail. Cowmen and townsmen were scurrying in and out of stores and a bedlam of excited words was tossed against the warm air like sand in a windstorm. Jack shouldered past dozens of small groups of alarmed citizens and made his way to the bank. Banker Yates was mopping his face with a damp handkerchief.

"Jack! Come into my office." Yates led the way in a bird-like, hopping walk. He dropped into a chair and waved a shaking hand toward another. Masters remained standing, waiting for the floodgates to open. They did, with a rush. "It wasn't more than an hour or so after you boys left town. There were three of them. One. . . ."

"Three of 'em?"

"Yes. Link Tolliver, the ferry keeper, and two others."

"Oh. Go on."

"They knew what they were doing. It didn't take them ten minutes to force our two safes and loot the place. A cashier named Reedy drew on them and was shot down. He's over behind the counter yet. It was terrible, Jack. They robbed Dennis's general store and the Goldstrike Saloon, too. Mendocino's ruined, I tell you. We'll never. . . ."

"All right, Yates, get a hold of yourself. Figger up your losses an' calm down."

The Goldstrike had pretty much the same story to tell, as did Mike Dennis, corpulent, furious owner of the Mendocino General Store and Emporium. Jack verified the robbers in each case. Link Tolliver and two other men. He nodded and described the other Tollivers to each irate victim. It was two of the three Tollivers he had met the day before at Cobb's Ferry. Wes Flourney came up, gloomy-faced, and Jack nodded before the deputy could speak.

"He's gone. I know. It was Link that led the raid. Link and two other Tollivers. Round up the posse we came in with, Wes, and we'll hit the trail. Don't take any more men than the four cowboys. Too many'll only slow us down. Bring the horses and the posse up to the office, I'll meet you there."

It didn't take Flourney long to round up the posse on their freshly saddled horses and the five of them rode up to the office where Jack Masters, wearing a freshly filled cartridge belt, mounted on the fly, and they swept out of Mendocino, heading south, down the road the bandits had taken.

Jack was somber-eyed as he loped after the Tollivers. He knew that failure to apprehend the renegades would spell the finish to his career as sheriff of Mendocino County. Through no fault of his own, he had been outwitted—not once, but twice. Local anger needed either a scapegoat or a hero—which he would be, one way or the other, since he was the acknowledged leader of the law-abiding sector.

He shrugged gloomily. With a two-hour start, it wasn't very likely that he would find his men that day, and only a stroke of luck would allow him to find them at all. He looked back, into the bitter, savage faces of the four cowmen riding as his posse. Beside deputy Flourney was young Bud Prouty, whose father was badly wounded and his brother dead because of the Tollivers. There was assurance and comfort in the stubborn gleam from Bud's narrowed eyes. If the others dropped out, which he expected before the chase was over, he, Wes, and Bud would keep on riding until they were either riding over the Tolliver bodies or the Tollivers were riding over theirs. He swung forward again and studied the freshest tracks on the road.

It wasn't hard to follow the barefoot marks of the Tolliver animals. He had been riding for an hour when he suddenly yanked up his horse, puzzled and frowning.

Flourney kneed up close. "What's the matter?"

"Lost 'em, Wes. No more barefoot hoof marks." He swung his horse around and the others followed as he trotted back the way they had come, bending low in the saddle, watching closely for the spot in the road where the Tollivers had veered off. At that, Jack and Wes missed it. Bud Prouty gave a small cry and pointed to a faint trail of bent, dry grass and churned-up earth. All six of them studied the tracks gravely, then reined out over the plain in a slow lope, eyes down and narrowed with the effort of watching for the telltale signs. One of the cowmen let out a string of profanity as they leaned a little northwest.

"I got it figgered. They're headin' back fer the ferry to pick up that dead 'un. 'Course, they don't know the buzzard's dead. Maybe he was s'posed to meet 'em, didn't, an' now they're goin' back to fetch him."

Wes bobbed his head soberly and looked over questioningly at Masters. "How's that sound, Jack?"

"Good, boys. Wes, you an' Bud Prouty cut off from us here an' ride hell for leather fer Cobb's Ferry. Be awful careful they don't ambush you. Don't close with 'em if you see 'em . . . just hold 'em up a little until we get there. Just in case this is a sour

29

guess, we'll stick to trailin' 'em. If they aren't at the ferry, you boys come on back an' trail us. *¿Comprende?*"

"*Si, jefe, si.*" Wes nodded to Bud, whose ashen face was getting a little color back with the possibility that they might close with the killers. Let's ride, cowboy!"

The dirt flew as the two younger men cut loose and charged down across the flat grassy range where an occasional clump of brush broke the monotony of the everlasting sameness. Jack watched them go with a level, approving gaze. When Wes and Bud were small specks in the distance, Masters and the other two went back to trotting slowly along, eyes glued to the frequent toe marks made by the running, barefoot horses. The sun was high now with exhilarating warmth that ate into bone and muscles with a soothing life-giving benevolence. They had been following the tracks in a steady, hesitant trot for some time when the faint report of a gun came down the wind to them. One of the cowmen swore and jerked in the saddle. "Comin' from Cobb's Ferry."

Jack listened closely, heard nothing, and nodded to the cowmen. "Let's ride, boys. Wes an' Bud are up ahead somewhere an' I reckon that was either a signal or an ambush. In either case we're needed." He flicked his spurred heels lightly and his horse jumped out with an eager lunge. Like four avenging angels they swung down across the land, slit-eyed and braced against the slipstream of warm air that slid over and past them. Two more shots came back to them and almost by instinct their horses gave an extra spurt of speed that sent them careening faster over the tundra.

# IV

A single shot, thunderous and violent, ripped the quiet atmosphere to shreds. The riders reined to a sliding halt. Two of the older men ducked involuntarily; one of them swore heartily. "That there's a rifle, boys. We better hit the dirt. Feller makes one helluva fine target up on top o' a horse."

The others were dismounting as he spoke. Masters edged forward, leading his horse. He came out on the high side of the slope leading down to the ferry just as the rifles blasted again from a corner of the building and an answering shot came from the brushy lip about 100 yards from Jack. He turned and motioned to the others to leave their horses and come in. One of the cowmen yanked his carbine from the boot; the others followed suit as Jack palmed his .30-30 and gave his horse a gentle slap, heading it back away from danger.

Death scored the first kill for the opposition. One of the cowmen was a little careless coming through the brush. The hidden rifleman rolled his rifle to bear on the dusty Stetson and squeezed off a shot that echoed and re-echoed over the deadly range, and one of the sheriff's company threw up his hands and went over in a heap, to hang lifelessly across a thick, thorny bush.

For a long time there was no firing. Jack and his two companions laid the dead man on the ground in a small clearing. If there had been a shred of mercy in them before, it was gone in an instant. They crawled cautiously forward as Bud Prouty and Wes fired twice, almost in unison, and a large chunk of old adobe flew out of the edge of the old building. A furious fusillade drove the posse to earth. The Tollivers were cornered because they had returned for their kinsman, but, desperate or not, they were all joining in the fight with deadly intent. When Jack risked a shot, he was immediately answered by the well-protected renegades. Apparently each of the remaining three Tollivers was armed with a rifle.

The posse men took advantage of a lull to creep down through the brush a little closer. Suddenly a concentrated fire erupted from the adobe. Jack sensed intuitively that the cornered men were fighting for time, hoping to hold off the attackers until nightfall would give them a chance to escape. Someone called out suddenly, and Jack turned his head. It was Wes Flourney and there was urgent desperation in his voice. Jack swore irritably and began the arduous crawl to his deputy. Emerging from the brush, torn and scratched, he and his companions saw Bud Prouty, bloody and unconscious, lying in a grotesque heap.

"Jack! Bud's got it bad. We gotta get him to Mendocino or he'll die."

Jack crawled over in silence and looked at the puffy little bluish puncture in Bud's upper body. He nodded gravely and turned to the two remaining posse men. "You boys take him in. It'll take both of you to hold him steady in the saddle."

Wes frowned in protest. "That'll only leave you an' me, Jack."

The sheriff shrugged. "Can't be helped, Wes. One man can't hold him on a horse an' it's a damned sight more important that he don't die than that the Tollivers get caught. It's a rough choice, but its gotta be that way." He swung his head to the posse men. "Get goin' boys. Every second counts. Fer gosh sakes don't drop him."

The cowmen were grim-faced as they carried the last of the Proutys through the brush. As soon as their hunched forms appeared over the thicket, rifle fire sent winging messengers of death slashing into the sage and manzanita. Jack watched them until they were out of sight, then he swung back to Wes. "Come on, kid. We're the whole damned posse now."

Together they wormed they way through the thicket until they were back on the overhanging slope where the dead man was lying, sightless, glazed eyes on the clear sky overhead. Wes took a quick, startled look, turned away quickly, and shoved his rifle forward.

Sheriff Masters searched for a worthwhile target. In this speculative, unhurried existence, he used his bullets as sparingly as his words. There wasn't any movement down below. Wes sighted at the edge of the porch and let drive. Two thunderous replies came immediately back from the edge of the house. Jack grunted a little, a perplexed frown on his face.

"Shoot down there again, Wes." The deputy aimed closer this time and squeezed off a round. Again the twin rifles snarled back, snipping the brush close by. Jack nodded thoughtfully. "That's bad. I don't like it."

"What?"

"Only two of 'em firin' now. Where's the third one?"

Wes looked apprehensively around and squinted down at the adobe. "Maybe we got one of 'em."

Masters shook his head. "The last time we traded slugs, they were all three shootin'. Now only two of 'em are shootin'."

Wes looked up at the descending sun and uncertainty began to reflect itself in his face. "Be hell of a note if they got away. Two slips in one day is bad enough, but we won't be real popular if they get away, too." He threw another shot into the adobe and drew two quick replies. Jack let his .30-30 slip out of his hand and shoved himself to his hands and knees.

"Where you goin'?"

"I'm goin' to try an' finish this thing before it gets so dark they can get past us. You keep on firin' every once in a while. Try an' get one of 'em, if you can. It'll make it a lot easier from my end."

"But, Jack, one man's in a poor way to do much down there. Hell, they'll kill. . . ."

"Maybe. I'll make 'em damned well earn it, Wes. You stay up here an' make 'em think we're both here. Be careful."

Flourney watched the sheriff disappear in the copse ahead of him. He was white-faced now as he glowered down at the house, looking for a halfway target. There was none. For a long, uneasy while there was silence, then someone down in the house let go an exploratory shot. Wes cocked his rifle, sighted for a long moment, then relaxed and let the gun barrel droop. The silence was nerve-wracking. Two quick shots whipped into the underbrush far to the left. Wes still didn't fire back. His eyes held a crafty, exultant gleam in them as the shadows grew longer.

He almost smiled when a side of a face came around the battered adobe house, sighting down a shiny Winchester barrel. Still he held his fire. The full face came into view and Wes figured about where the forehead would be, under the low Stetson's floppy brim. He drew a careful bead but didn't fire. The face disappeared briefly and Wes looked anxious. A man stepped into view, his rifle at the ready. Flourney lowered his head carefully, picked up the body over his sights. His finger was tightening over the trigger when a violent explosion down in front of him, in the brush, shook his nerve and he ducked without firing. Angrily he saw his target lunge out of sight behind the house.

Jack had reached the lower fringe of brush at the base of the slope behind Cobb's Ferry. He was prone and slit-eyed as he surveyed the nearby adobe house. He wanted to find some way of getting in close, but the clearing immediately around the adobe was devoid of any cover at all. Crossing it, even in a zigzag run, would be the equivalent of a lead-embroidered death certificate. He rolled over and looked back up the hill toward the hiding place of his deputy. Horror made a grimace out of his normally composed features. Coming noiselessly through the brush toward Wes was one of the Tollivers. The assassin held a cocked six-gun in his grimy paw, and Jack caught infrequent glimpses of the sweat-stained, dirty Stetson and the crouched-over shoulders. He knew that Flourney was lying there blissfully unaware that death was staking him with an implacable certainty.

Masters rolled recklessly backward and came up to one knee. The brush shook violently but that was a chance he had to take. A bullet in the back wasn't half as bad as being forced to sit back and watch the slaughter of his deputy. He aimed back up the hill, hunkered over his carbine, and let his finger rest caressingly over the trigger. The hunched-over figure appeared briefly, sideways, as the killer dodged into a small clearing. Jack breathed a very brief prayer and pinched the trigger. The Tolliver bushwhacker disappeared in a flurry of threshing limbs. A wild, shrill, and abandoned scream chilled the listeners on the slope and in the house.

Wes scrambled furiously back toward the victim, cocked .45 in hand. Fury burned in him like a consuming flame. He had not only lost the only worthwhile target he had seen during the entire fracas, but the scream had startled him into a cold sweat. He emerged into the clearing where the dead posse man lay and glowered at the smashed head of a stranger who he knew to be a Tolliver. Reluctantly he turned around and crawled back to his rifle, grabbed it in a hard fist, and began a swift descent of the brushy slope.

Jack was in a position where he could see the three saddled horses tied to the old log corral. It made him feel more confident, even though the shadows were lengthening at an alarming rate. He scooped up a rock and flung it overhand toward the house. The ruse didn't work. He skirted through the brush as far as he dared and gained a slight sideways view of the porch; ejected brass cartridge cases caught and reflected the dying rays of the sun like scattered nuggets of gold. There wasn't much time left, and the sheriff had a reputation at stake. He arose to a crouch, dropped the carbine, and drew his six-gun. For a long second he hesitated, then he began a wary, inanely reckless charge across the clearing toward the edge of the house.

Wes Flourney was unaware of the sheriff's charge toward the adobe until he heard the close crash of two guns nearby. One was a rifle and the other a deeper, less piercing belch of a short-barreled six-gun. He wanted to risk a peek but dropped flat instead. None of the slugs bludgeoned into the brush within hearing distance and the deputy correctly assumed that they were aimed at the sheriff, not him. He came up to one knee, held his six-gun ready, and risked a quick peek.

Jack had swapped point-blank fire with Link Tolliver. He had recognized the big paunchy figure before one of the renegade's bullets crumpled his right leg to support him as he limped forward, three slugs still left in his hot gun.

Suddenly Link Tolliver appeared on the porch; he had two heavy saddlebags thrown over his massive shoulder and a defiant, crazy look on his face. He had made a decision. Either he shot his way clear or he went to hell with the Mendocino loot still in his possession. Jack Masters leveled and fired once. Tolliver sagged, forced himself upright, and began an inexorable walk toward the sheriff. There was a ghastly smile on his sweat-streaked face, a wild, animal snarl. His gun belched twice in quick succession. Jack felt the burn of the slug over his hip. He was dimly conscious of the sticky warmth that was running down the inside leg of his pants to pour into his boot.

He raised his gun barrel a little and squeezed the trigger. The heavy walnut butt slammed into his palm. Link Tolliver stopped in mid-stride. The snarl of hate and challenge changed to a lopsided, crazy glare. He knew he was finished now. The second shot made a gorge of thick, salty blood rise in his throat. Still, there was no pain. He realized he'd never live to spend the heavy weight of the gold and silver that gouged into his fleshy shoulder, and he didn't care. Link Tolliver wanted just one thing on earth. That was to kill the representative of the law—of everything he loathed and despised—that was standing up, spraddle-legged, shooting it out with him.

He brought up his gun in a white, weakening fist; there was a red rim border to his eyesight that he tried to ignore. A mushroom of incredible brilliance exploded in his face; the salty taste in his throat was a torrent now. Sheriff Jack Masters had methodically shot his last shell. Link's gun wavered. The barrel drooped, the great body sobbed once, and a rush of blood broke past the slackening lips and cascaded down the grimy shirt. The big renegade went down slowly, gracefully; he fought off going with every bit of his remaining strength. When the body hit the warped old planking, Jack could feel the reverberation all the way over to where he stood on one good leg.

With the grim singleness of purpose that made the old-time sheriffs great and respected, Jack Masters went slowly forward until he was over the fallen Tolliver. He stooped and painfully picked up the dead man's gun, saw that two bullets remained in the cylinder, and dragged his lacerated leg after him toward the open door of the house. He stopped just outside the opening and there were little beads of painful sweat popping out on his forehead.

"Come out, *hombre,* or I'll come in after you an' we'll go to hell together."

There was no answer, and Jack made a crazy lurch that brought his gory, ragged form into the doorway. He was crouched and holding back the trigger of Tolliver's warm gun. His thumb was already sliding off the hammer when a muscular convulsion stayed the deadly digit. There was a foolish look on his face. His voice came out cracked and rasping: "Who are you?"

"Jessica Tolliver, Link's sister. I came here to try an' talk them out of it. It's always been the same. Trouble an' bloodshed." The voice was rich, even in its agony and pathos. "They wouldn't listen." A pert, oval of a face with monumental suffering writhing in the dark depths of the cobalt eyes swung up to Jack. "Go ahead, Sheriff. I have a gun. Shoot me."

"Jessica." The voice was husky. Something jolting had struck Jack under the heart somewhere. He had never had it happen before. It was crazy that it should hit him there and then, while the still warm blood of her dead brother and kinsmen was even then congealing only a few feet away.

"Jessica, drop the gun. Stand trial, Jessica."

The girl shook her head and a wealth of taffy hair glinted under the dove-gray Stetson as her full bosom rose and fell irregularly under the sudden impact of a weak, delicious agony that ran wildly within her as their eyes locked. "What's your name, Sheriff?"

"Jack. Jack Masters."

"No, Jack. It's too late for the trial." There was an almost desperate wistfulness in her voice and eyes as she walked over close and looked up into the sheriff's face, drawn and white with weakness and pain.

"Oh, Jack, I've had one awfully brief glance of what might have been tonight. I didn't think it would ever happen, and now"—her round arm waved in a hard, frustrated little circle that covered the embattled ground of Cobb's Ferry—"it not only did happen, but here, where there's death."

A slight sob echoed in her throat. She raised quickly on the toes of her boots, brushed a quick, soft little kiss over Jack's mouth, and went out the door, off the porch, and down toward the horse corral. Jack, remembering suddenly, frantically, that Wes Flourney was out there somewhere, dropped his gun and lurched outside to yell a warning. His mouth was still open and wordless when the snarling blast of a single shot rang out. Jessica Tolliver took two faltering little steps, and fell.

Jack Masters ran drunkenly over the ragged earth where the

long evening shadows were blotting out the devastation of the spent, blood-drenched day. He went down beside her and lifted her head. There was a raw bruise on her forehead and a welter of rich, vital blood was trickling from the valley between her breasts, high up near the top button of her shirt. "Jessica. . . ."

"You, Jack?" There wasn't a shred of reproach in the words. Wonder, maybe, but no accusation. He shook his head.

"No, Jessie. My deputy. He couldn't tell in the dusk. He didn't know, Jessie."

"Is it bad, Jack?"

He bit back the acid that erupted in his throat and nodded his head gently. She smiled up at him. There was a peaceful finality on her face and she reached up shakily and dropped one small, dimpled hand over his filthy knuckles. "Jack, if I save a place beside me, up there, will you look for it when you ride over?"

Again he nodded. "Yes, Jessie. Save a place for me. I'll be along. Wait for me, Jessie, promise?" She sighed a little and nodded, her moist, large eyes on his with a deep abiding faithfulness. They were dimming now and Jack's soul was wrenched hard when the honey-colored hair fell loosely over his arm with a solemn, final grace.

The ride back to Mendocino was like the return of two wraiths. The darkness hid most of the brush scratches, the ragged, torn clothing, and the sunken-eyed, bone weariness. It hid the little string of rack horses that plodded patiently along behind Jack's and his deputy's horses. But all the darkness in the world couldn't hide the soggy, plumping sounds as the corpses, lashed sideways over the saddles, bumped and lurched against the ropes that held them, taking their last ride on a horse.

The light of a new day made a difference. Yates had his blood-stained money from Link's saddlebags and Bud Prouty was mending as well as could be expected. Mendocino's boothill boasted of several new graves, but one grave, at the thin-lipped stubborn insistence of the sheriff, had been put apart. It was a better grave, too. There were flowers and a prayer and a silent renewal of a promise lying over it like an aura.

Mendocino was proud of her sheriff. There were triumphant celebrations and fireworks, and Jack Masters smiled his way through it all, the same old Jack, just a little quieter, perhaps, a little grayer in the face, and a little less willing to laugh, but to the cowmen and the townsmen these things went unnoticed and ignored. To them he was their conquering hero.

★ ★ ★ ★ ★

# Vermilion Kid

★ ★ ★ ★ ★

# I

To a man from a cesspool, the gutter is heaven. Those were the
words. He turned the whiskey glass around and around in its
own little sticky pool of clear liquid on the bar top, and thought
of them. If a man had said them, he'd have killed him—shot
him down with the ferocious fury of a self-made gunman.
Called, drawn, and shot, all with the unbelievable speed that
had made him feared, hated, and fawned over the width of the
raw, rude frontier.

But it hadn't been a man, it was a girl—a slip of a woman at
that. Not over 110 pounds of fragile, violet-eyed, taffy-haired
girl. The kind that made heroes out of their men while they
themselves lived and died unsung. A real Western woman.

He couldn't get the words out of his mind; they were sort of
poetic. *To a man from a cesspool, the gutter is heaven.* Why, damn
her, anyway. Her father was Buff Dodge. Big, wealthy, gruff,
and friendly—one of the richest cowmen in the whole wide
West, which, of course, meant the whole damned world. To hell
with her old man and his money. The Vermilion Kid was pretty
famous, too. And he had money—although no one but himself
knew it.

He slid the whiskey glass along, making the little pool take
on an oblong, roughly heart-shaped outline. He knew what
she'd meant, though. He nodded slightly, morosely. There was a
difference all right, sure there was. He was an outlaw. That the
law had never caught him didn't alter the facts one damned bit.

She knew it, and he knew it, and, he surmised tartly, so did the whole damned world. Even so, it sure hurt, when he'd tried to scrape up an acquaintanceship to have her drown it with a sentence like that. He downed the whiskey and turned bitterly away from the bar.

The First Chance saloon was a bedlam of noise, pungent odors of tobacco, liquor, and human sweat. The Vermilion Kid grinned wryly, sourly to himself as he made his way through the press of raucous, writhing bodies to the faro table. He gambled with his usual indifferent luck and the warmth of the room—generated by the hissing, glaring lanterns, the feverish, recklessly hilarious patrons, and the dingy, worn little iron stove in a far corner—made a small wreath of sweaty beads stand out on his upper lip and his forehead. His slate gray eyes were somber, constantly moving over the room with a liquid, smooth movement and a look of sardonic ridicule had settled over his tanned, lean cheeks.

He marshaled his chips and counted them unconsciously, always aware of the toss of that taffy hair and the proud, piquant face, and then the dagger of the words spanked up hard against the back of his forehead.

*To a man from a cesspool, the gutter is heaven.* He quit the game, had another drink, and stalked out of the saloon. The night was warm and clear, with little tremors of coolness settling down on the earth after the vicious heat of the day. He went to the Royal House, hiked the stairs to his room, locked the door very carefully, and went to the bed with the same ten words of contempt drenching him with their frigid repugnance.

At breakfast the following morning, the Vermilion Kid's badly mauled pride had shielded itself behind a mask of indifference, as it always did. In fact, he was pretty well along in the process of forgetting the whole damned episode—or so he told himself, when the hotel clerk came up to his table. He was the only occupant of the dining room and the man clearly showed that he had to talk to someone. The Kid motioned to a chair as the clerk hesitated. "Sit down." The clerk sat with a slight, self-conscious nod of thanks.

"Sure's too bad, ain't it?"

The Kid knew the routine. He was supposed to look up, perplexed, and ask what was too bad? He shrugged instead, deliberately, and pointed to his thick plate of ham and eggs. "You had breakfast?"

The clerk was deflated. "Ain't hungry." He tried a more natural approach. "You hear what happened last night?"

"Nope, don't reckon I did." He continued to fork the food into his mouth.

"Some cowboys ridin' back out of town come across ol' man Dodge's body, plumb shot all to hell an' stiffer'n a ramrod, about two miles out o' town."

At the name of Dodge, the Kid's soft, nervous fingers laid aside his eating utensils. His gray eyes came up smoky and he chewed methodically until he swallowed, looking at the clerk. "Well, what's the rest of it?" There was a sudden earnestness in his voice that the clerk didn't fail to recognize. He shrugged, anti-climatically.

"Ain't nothin' more. Them riders jus' found the old guy shot to death, that's all." The last came tartly, a little indignantly, as though the clerk resented the Kid's calm, steady eye and relaxed manner. He excused himself, got up, turned with a slight frown, and walked out of the dining room.

For possibly fifteen seconds the Kid didn't move, then he got up, pulled his hat absently onto his head, flipped a ragged piece of paper money on the table, and walked out of the hotel into the blast furnace sunlight that was firing its molten wrath down upon Holbrook. Without seeing, he looked up and down the lone, ragged, unkempt street and turned toward the livery barn.

A hostler got his horse and the Kid saddled up, mounted, flipped a piece of change to the whiskey-wrecked old sot who had gotten his horse, and rode out of the barn. He turned down the hot roadway with its tiny, whirling dust devils that jerked to life under his big black gelding's freshly shod hoofs, and out of Holbrook, heading north, toward the vast D-Back-To-Back, the Dodge Ranch. The bleary-eyed hostler looked from the coin in his hand to the disappearing rider and his filmy eyes were incredulous. He held a $20 gold piece in his hand—more money than he'd had since he'd been a top rider for the 101, nearly fifteen years before. Twenty golden dollars to hide in his filthy rags until it burned a livid hole in his pocket that'd match the searing ache in his ravished body for whiskey.

As the Kid rode toward the tremendous Dodge holdings, his mind went bitterly, fleetingly to the ten little words that had hurt worse than anything that'd been said to, or about, him since he'd carved his own violent, mysterious arc across the firmament of the frontier. He more than suspected that his intended offer would be bluntly, savagely refused by Toma Dodge. Still, he wanted to make it—perhaps so she'd hurt him again. He wasn't sure why, but he fully intended to make the offer anyway.

As the Kid rode leisurely toward his destiny, back in Holbrook there was an explosive and profane council going on in Sheriff Dugan's office. Emmett Dugan was gray and grizzled, hard and indifferent to everything except his job as sheriff of Concho County. He was a brooding bachelor, fiery of tongue and rough in appearance. The man opposite him was articulate, dark, and handsome in an oily, unprepossessing way.

"I don't know when he come in, Sheriff. This mornin', when I got down to the barn, Bob had put him in a stall and doctored him. He's down there now, if you want to see him."

Dugan got up slowly. "Well, let's go look. Don't see how the dang' critter can be alive, though, if he's shot like you say."

Side-by-side the big forbidding-looking sheriff and his smaller, immaculate-looking companion walked down the protesting plank sidewalk to the livery barn. The dark man led up to a gloomy stall where a powerful bay horse stood forlornly in a shadowy corner, head down, lower lip hanging, breathing with bubbling, rasping sounds. The marks of a recently removed saddle were still outlined on the beast's back. Dugan opened the stall door and went up to the wounded horse. Les Tallant, the livery barn owner, went in with him and pointed to a ragged, swollen, and purplish hole.

"Right through the chest." His voice was unconsciously lowered. The horse didn't look up. Dugan walked around the horse, studying the wounds. The animal had been struck a little forward of the left front shoulder. Already a bloody scab had formed over the torn, swollen flesh. Dugan walked softly over the straw bedding around to the other side, shaking his head. He looked thoughtfully at the hole in the wounded saddle animal for a second time, then turned and went out of the stall. Tallant followed him out, latching the door behind him.

"It's Buff Dodge's big bay, all right. I'd know that horse anywhere. He prob'ly ambled into town an' come to your barn because he remembered that's where Buff used to leave him when he come to town. Damn." The sheriff shook his head wearily, sadly. "Ol' Buff was one o' my best friends." That was as close as Emmett Dugan ever came to showing emotion.

Les Tallant wagged his head back and forth a little and the opaque black eyes were impassive. " 'Course, Dodge carried money on him, usually more than was wise . . . but, dammit all, it's hard to think of anyone who'd kill him to get it."

"Oh, I don't know, Tallant. They's two kinds of owlhooters. They's the kind that'll hold a man up fer his *dinero*, an' then

47

there's the kind that'll kill to rob. Mostly these latter kind know the man they're robbin' an' don't want no witnesses . . . or else they're just plain killers at heart. It was one of these here kind that killed Buff."

Tallant was soberly quiet for a few seconds before he answered. "Yeah, I reckon you're right." He shrugged slightly. "Well, what you want me to do with the critter?"

Dugan was shuffling out of the livery barn as he spoke. "Jus' leave him there. I don't allow he'll make it, anyway, from the looks of them holes, so jus' leave him where he can die in peace." He was out of the barn when he finished speaking and he turned toward his office without a backward look. Les Tallant watched him go thoughtfully, then walked slowly over to the Royal House for his breakfast.

# II

There was a huge old wooden gate that had the D-Back-To-Back burned deeply into its crossbar where the road swung past and the Vermilion Kid rode through it. His big black horse was ambling along sleepily and the Kid appraised the little bunches of cattle he saw here and there as he followed the well-worn ranch road. The beef looked good. Of course, there were a few old cows whose bones showed, but they all had big, fat calves by their sides. Mostly, though, the cattle were fat as ticks and placidly contented.

The buildings were old, weather-beaten, but well kept up. The house alone was painted and its verandah ran completely around it, shading the outer walls. An assortment of old, cane-bottomed chairs and a hammock or two were in the shade. There was the clear, clarion ringing of a man working at an anvil and the sound, musical and strident, rode down the hot summer air to the Kid as he rode up to a log hitch rail before the house, swung down, and tied up.

There was no sign of human activity among the buildings, and, except for the unseen smithy, the ranch might have been deserted. The Kid's spurs tinkled softly as he walked across the cool, shadowy verandah and knuckled the door. While he waited, the Kid looked at the gray old pole corrals and the huge log barn, all tight and solid. He felt a glow of appreciation. Here was a Western ranch where you didn't have to strain your innards every time you opened a gate. That was as it should be, but all too seldom—it wasn't the way things were kept, generally speaking. His musings were interrupted and he turned back as the door swung open. The Kid's hat came off and he was standing face to face with a small, full-bodied, and red-eyed woman. Toma Dodge. For an instant she looked up at him blankly, then recognition swept over her face. He could feel the wall of antagonism building up between them.

"Please, Miss Dodge, I'm sorry about yesterday. It won't happen again."

"Is that what you rode all the way out here to say?"

He shook his head. "No, ma'am. I heard about your father an' I came out to offer my help in any way you want to use it." He said it exactly as he had rehearsed it. It was better to be diplomatic than to come right out and say he was a lethal killer and would gladly gun down the murderers of her father. This way she might let him help.

There was a flash of anger through the anguish in her face. She tossed her small, taffy-colored head in that mannerism he remembered so well and the words cut deeply. "Thank you, Mister Vermilion Kid, but I think one encounter with renegades, in the past twenty-four hours, has proven disastrous enough for my family. I don't think I want to chance another accident." The way she said "accident" made the Kid squirm inwardly. He stood in silent anger for a long moment, just looking down into the wide violet eyes. Then the anger dropped away and he nodded twice, curtly and softly.

"I knew it was foolish to come out here and offer my services. I knew you'd say something like that." He put his dusty black Stetson on with an unconscious gesture. "Well, Miss Dodge, I hope someday you learn to judge people better."

He turned abruptly and started across the verandah toward his horse. He knew she was watching him, because he didn't hear the door close. A man's gruff voice came to him as he untied the horse, and, despite his resolve not to look up, he did anyway.

A blunt-jawed individual was standing next to the wisp of a girl in the doorway, glowering down at him. The Kid flipped his reins, turned his horse a little, and had one foot in the stirrup when he heard the man's spurs ringing across the verandah, coming toward him.

He was about to swing aboard when a surly voice spoke behind him: "Don't let me catch you trespassin' on the D-Back-To-Back again, mister."

The Kid's foot slid easily out of the stirrup and he turned slowly. His eyes were level with the angry brown eyes when he spoke softly: "I don't believe I know you, *hombre.*"

"Jeff Beale, foreman of the D-Back-To-Back. I'm the one who gives the orders hereabouts, *hombre,* an' I'm tellin' you not to set foot on this here range again."

Normally the Kid might have overlooked the man's big talk, but now there were two reasons why he didn't. One was the girl still standing in the shadowy doorway, and two was the discomfort and hurt of her words. In short, the Vermilion Kid had absorbed about all the unpleasantness a man could accommodate in so short a space of time. He didn't answer at all, but his gloved fist dropped behind the slope of his shoulder in a flashing fraction of a quick second, then arose with the mauling, bruising weight of his whipcord body behind it. If the foreman saw it coming, he made no move to get away. The fist chopped and popped like a bullwhip when it connected with his square jaw. Jeff Beale went over backward like a pole-axed steer.

The Kid swung back toward the girl. "I don't know why, Miss Dodge, but every time I try to talk to you there's trouble." His voice was calm and his smoke-gray eyes were mildly puzzled. "I'm sorry about this"—he jutted his chin toward the inert form of Beale—"but you're a witness that I didn't start it." Seeing that the girl was listening and looking at him in silence, he took another plunge. "I wish you'd let me help you. I've been around things like this before an' maybe I could do some good. At any rate, I'd sure like to try."

For the first time since he'd known her, her voice wasn't ringing with pure contempt when she spoke. "And if I agreed, what would your pay be?"

He admired her common sense and couldn't help but smile a little lopsidedly. "Nothin', ma'am. I don't want your money. Just agree to let me sleep in the bunkhouse an' eat with the other D-Back-To-Back men, that's all."

Her eyes went to the gently stirring form of Jeff Beale. "Help him up and we'll talk about it."

Beale stood on wobbly legs and ran an exploratory hand over his bruised jaw. He was listening to Toma Dodge, but his squinted eyes were thoughtfully on the blank, unsmiling face of the Vermilion Kid. Finally he nodded. "All right, Toma, if that's what you want, we'll try it, but. . . ." The brown eyes were perplexed and Beale shook his head. "Hell, I don't know. I guess we can try him out, anyway."

The Kid rode back to Holbrook, stuffed his scanty gear into his saddlebags, paid his bill at the Royal House, and returned to the D-Back-To-Back. When he was putting up his horse, three cowboys sauntered over to the corral and watched him in impassive silence. He nodded, and the riders nodded back. The Kid had been a cowboy once and he knew what the men were doing. They were appraising him—evaluating his appearance, his tack and his horse; from these things they would deduce his status among them.

Apparently the silent judgment was favorable because he was gradually included in the men's jokes and hazing until, after two days on the ranch, the Vermilion Kid was more at home than he had been in many years. Jeff Beale introduced him to the men. At the sound of his name, there was a startled, awkward silence that, strangely enough, Beale himself filled in with casual talk until the riders got over their furtive stares and sudden silence.

For two days the Kid worked the cattle with the men. He saw neither Toma Dodge nor Beale, except in the early morning when the foreman would line out the work. The Kid was anxious to work on the murder, and the evening of the third day he went up to the house. Toma admitted him to a huge old parlor with a roaring fire in a massive, smoked-over old stone fireplace. He recognized the ancient trappings of the old frontier on the walls. Indian trophies hung droopily among old tintype pictures and the comfortable old leather furniture was typical of an earlier day on the frontier. The Kid held his hat self-consciously in his hand and turned it by the brim in slow, nervous convolutions as he spoke. "Miss Dodge, it sort of seems to me like we're wastin' a lot of good time."

The girl nodded, her eyes on the colorful Navajo rugs. "I know, it seems like that to me, too, but Jeff is nosing around in Holbrook and doesn't want you to do anything until he's chased down some ideas he has about Dad's murder."

The Kid frowned. His answer was dryly matter-of-fact. "Well, while Beale's lookin' around, a lot of water can pass under the bridge."

The beautiful eyes came up with a decisive upsweep of the head. "I know it, Kid. You can start out on your own tomorrow, only. . . ."

"Only . . . what?"

"Only don't let Jeff know what you're doing. He'll be angry if he knows I let you start your investigation."

The Kid's eyebrows came together over his steady gray eyes. "Miss Dodge, this here's likely to be a long drawn-out an' dangerous little chore. Don't you think we ought to start out by trustin' each other?"

"What do you mean?" Her face colored a little.

"Well, if Beale doesn't know what I'm up to, it'll make a lot of unnecessary hard feelings, won't it?"

Toma Dodge stood up and looked at the fireplace. The Kid felt a sudden little tug at his heartstrings as he studied her profile. She was so small and helpless-looking, yet so much a woman, the kind of a woman a man needed. "I don't know what to say."

The Kid guessed, correctly, that her father's sudden demise had projected her into a role of responsibility that was altogether foreign, and a little frightening, to her. He got up and went over beside her, his hat gripped tightly in his hands. There was a half-wistful, half-truculent look on his face.

"All right, Miss Dodge. I'll keep out of Beale's way. We'll do it your way, but frankly I don't think it's too good an idea."

She turned toward him. For a wild second her eyes locked with his and a strong electric current passed between them. The Kid turned away in confusion and, mumbling excuses, left the house. Outside, the stars were clear and brittle. He rolled and smoked a cigarette in the warm, velvety shadows of the corrals. He didn't think it would ever happen, but it had; he was in love.

# III

At daybreak, the Vermilion Kid had saddled up and ridden out of the D-Back-To-Back ranch yard. The air was cool without being cold and the land was lazily stirring to life. Here and there a hustling rabbit was out searching for dew-drenched young shoots and garrulous, sleepy birds made slight noises at his passing. Holbrook was just coming to life when the Kid rode in. He left his horse at the livery stable. The bleary-eyed hostler smiled at him through a foul fog of sickening breath. "Sure nice to see you again."

The Kid raised his eyebrows. He had forgotten tipping the man so lavishly, besides, his mind was on a small, oval face with violet eyes. He smiled vacantly, said nothing, and walked slowly out of the barn. He was almost to the street when the hostler came weaving up to him. "Say, I was wonderin' if you'd he'p me move a horse?"

"Move one? Hell, can't you lead him?"

"No, y'see, this here critter's dyin' from a bullet wound an' he's down."

The Kid understood. The animal was down, weak and dying, and the hostler wanted to turn him over so his body weight would be on the off legs for a while; just in case he ever got up again, the legs wouldn't be too numb to operate. He walked back, helped the hostler turn the horse, straightened up, and was dusting off his hands when he saw the hip brand. D-Back-To-Back.

"Where'd you get this horse?"

"He come staggerin' in here the night Dodge was killed. 'Twas his horse, so the sheriff says."

The Kid studied the bullet holes with compressed lips, then walked from the barn. He went to the Royal House and had an early breakfast. The dining room was vacant and he ate slowly, turning Dodge's murder over in his mind.

The day was well along and the Kid had decided to have a talk with Sheriff Dugan. He was approaching the sheriff's office when he saw Dugan and Jeff Beale standing in the shade of the portico, watching him come forward. The Kid felt an uneasy suspicion at the silent, intent way they watched him approach, but shook it off. He was almost in front of the two men when his wary eye, trained from youth to be alert, caught the slight drop of Beale's right shoulder. The Kid halted, legs apart, surprised but not unprepared.

There was a long, tense silence, then Emmett Dugan, still motionless, spoke: "Don't go for it, Kid."

"No? Why not?"

"'Cause I want to talk to you, an' a killin' won't help you any right now."

"All right, Sheriff, tell Beale to shove his hands deep in his pockets."

Dugan turned to the D-Back-To-Back foreman. "Do like he says, Jeff."

Beale hesitated, still staring, wide-eyed, at the Kid.

"Come on, Jeff, gun play won't settle nothin' . . . not yet, anyway."

Beale shoved his balled-up fists reluctantly into his pockets, and the Kid approached warily until he was even with the two men. Dugan jerked a thumb toward his office, but the Kid slowly shook his head.

"Let's do our talkin' right here, Sheriff. I sort of like the fresh air this mornin'."

Dugan regarded the gunman for a long, doleful moment, then shrugged. "Kid, where was you the night Dodge got killed?"

"Early in the evenin' I was at the First Chance, later I went to bed in my room at the Royal House."

"Got any proof that you were abed?"

The Kid snorted. "Hardly, Sheriff. I make it a habit to sleep alone."

Dugan and Beale exchanged a significant glance, which the Kid saw. He puckered up his eyebrows and looked from one to the other. "Just what in hell have you two *hombres* got on your minds?"

Dugan spoke slowly, in a measured voice devoid of inflections, as if he was reciting a story. "Dodge was killed an' robbed. We got reason to suspect you done it. If you got proof you didn't, then we gotta hunt further afield. But if you ain't got proof, then I'm goin' to hold you for a while."

The Kid's right shoulder sagged perceptibly and his eyes narrowed. He shook his head slowly. "No, Sheriff, I didn't kill or rob Dodge, an' you're not goin' to hold me, either." His voice was almost gentle, and Beale looked at Dugan accusingly, hands still rammed into his pants pockets.

Dugan shifted his weight a little and frowned. "If you're innocent, Kid, you got nothin' to worry about. Better give me your gun."

"No good, Sheriff. I don't know what kind of a deal is cooked up here, but I'm not goin' to walk into a noose to help it along."

There was a long moment of silence as Dugan's flinty eyes washed over the Kid. He knew the Kid's reputation with a gun, but Emmett Dugan had a job and a duty to perform, and his complete lack of imagination saw only the course he must pursue. He shook his head slowly and his face set in hard, uncompromising lines. "I'm warnin' you, Kid, you got no choice."

"You're wrong, Sheriff"—the voice was very gentle now—"I got a pretty good choice."

Dugan almost sighed. The Kid saw his eyes widen a fraction of an inch. That was all he needed. Two explosions rocked the still, lazy atmosphere of Holbrook. There was a second of awful suspense, then twice more the coughing roar of a .45 blasted the silence. Dugan was cursing in a low, deadly monotone and sagged against the front of his office, holding a scarlet rag of torn shirt over his ribs and Jeff Beale, outgunned from scratch, was writhing in the dust of the roadway, a bullet through the hip. The Vermilion Kid was untouched and crouched low with his lips pressed back flat over his teeth.

Holbrook's citizens were prudent folk. They loved to revel in the recounting of gunfights, but they reasoned, logically enough, that in order to pass on the stories, it was a necessary requisite that one stay alive. In order to accomplish this, they stayed out of sight until the fight was over. Thus it was that the Vermilion Kid strolled away from the scene of carnage, retrieved his horse from the suddenly sobered hostler at the livery barn, and rode easily out of town in a long, mile-eating lope.

That night the Kid sat on a juniper-studded knoll that overlooked the D-Back-To-Back ranch house. The watery, faint light of the clear, cold stars and the weak moon, made shadows of the coming and going riders below. He knew that Toma Dodge had heard, by now, of his shooting scrape. He wondered what she thought of him, in light of his recent blunder. The Kid thoughtfully chewed a straw as the night hours drifted by. Finally, when the last lights had died out over the ranch, he carefully removed his spurs and made a cautious, laborious descent to the gloomy buildings of the ranch. The Kid got to the house without much trouble. The riders were sawing wood after the day's excitement. The Kid forced a window with determined effort, slid through the opening, only to feel the cold, menacing barrel of a six-gun in his belly. He exhaled slowly and tried to pierce the gloom.

"Don't move." It was Toma's voice.

The Kid froze but felt a surge of relief at the same time. At any rate, it wasn't Dugan or Beale. "Miss Dodge . . . ?"

"Be quiet. I should've known better than to trust you. I. . . ."

"Dog-gone it, hold on a minute, will you? I didn't have a chance. . . ."

The voice of the girl was as firm as the gun barrel. "No, of course you didn't. Oh, what a fool I was to believe in you. Jeff Beale suspected you from the start, and, when he found the bullet in Dad's horse, he and Sheriff Dugan stole one of your bullets and they matched. I ought to kill you right now. You're nothing but a cold-blooded murderer."

All the time she was talking, the Kid was trying to piece something together. He listened to her angry voice drone into the darkness without hearing much of what she said, then it came to him in a flash. He started to move and the gun barrel, momentarily forgotten, pressed deeper. He pulled backward instinctively and interrupted the flood of vituperation.

"Wait a minute, will you? Hold it a second." Her voice died away gradually, begrudgingly, and the Kid tried to see the violet eyes, but he couldn't. "Did you say Beale found a bullet in your paw's horse?"

"Yes. He dug it out this afternoon, after you shot him." Her voice held a full measure of sarcastic triumph in it. "He wasn't so badly shot up that Doc Carter didn't patch him up enough to go on digging up facts to hang you with."

The Kid's funny bone had been rubbed. He nodded soberly, lugubriously. "Yeah, I'm sure of it, ma'am, especially since I didn't shoot to kill . . . but just hold off pullin' that trigger for one second, will you?"

"Well?"

"Look, Toma. . . ."

"Miss Dodge!"

"Uh, yeah, Toma . . . uh, Miss Dodge, honey. Your dad's horse was shot through the chest sort of between the shoulders an' the chest. The bullet went in on the left side. There's a hole to show where it entered, an' on the right side there's a hole to show where it come out. Now, listen, Toma. . . ."

"Miss Dodge!"

"Uh, yeah, Toma, now listen. How in . . . uh, heck . . . could Beale dig the bullet out of your paw's horse, when the slug went in one side an' come out the other side? In other words, ma'am, there couldn't have been any slug in that there critter to dig out."

The girl was silent and the Kid felt the pressure on the gun barrel lessen slightly. She was silent so long that the Kid felt uneasy. "You didn't happen to see the horse, did you?"

"No."

"Was Sheriff Dugan here this evenin'?"

"Yes."

"Look, Toma"—there was pointed pause but she didn't take it up—"do me a favor, will you?"

"What?"

"Go to Holbrook tomorrow mornin' an' look at that there horse."

"Yes, I intend to . . . but not as a favor to you."

The gun-barrel had dropped quite a bit and the Kid wanted to smile.

"Well, then, can I go now?"

"Why did you come here tonight?"

"To talk to you, to tell you how I was forced to make that gun play or get locked up, an' I don't want to get locked up just yet. I've got a couple of ideas I want to try out. Can I go now?"

The gun was at her side now, dangling from a white, small hand. Out of place and slightly ridiculous. She tried to see his eyes in the darkness. "You haven't discovered anything, then?"

The Kid gingerly let one leg out of the window as he answered. "Yes, ma'am, I discovered one thing. 'Course, it's got no bearin' that I can see on the murder, but still it's awful important to me."

"What is it?"

"That I'm in love with you."

He was gone over the windowsill before she could recover from the surprise and shock. The faint rustle of his boot heels in the geranium bed softly blended into the night and Toma Dodge sank into a rocker and let the gun drop to the floor. She let her wan, worried face follow the shadowy figure that faded into the gloom as the Vermilion Kid fled through the night, back to his patiently grazing big black horse on the little knoll.

# IV

The Kid was in his element now and there were few better at it. He was on the dodge. There were handbills tacked to the trees along the Holbrook road and on the fronts of buildings in town. He hid with the almost nonchalant casualness of an old hand on the owlhoot trail. Once he even slipped into Holbrook. He flattened against the walls of the livery barn and buttonholed the startled hostler.

"Listen, pardner, I want you to tell me somethin'."

The hostler recognized him and relaxed a little. He hadn't forgotten that $20 gold piece. "Sure, Kid, what is it?"

"Was Beale alone when he dug a slug out of Dodge's horse?"

"Well, I don't know what he done to the horse, 'cause they sent me away. . . ."

"Who were they?"

"Oh, Les Tallant . . . the *hombre* who owns this here barn . . . an' Jeff Beale. They was messin' around that wounded horse, an', when I come up, Tallant told me to beat it. I don't know what they done to the poor critter after I left."

"How is the horse?"

" 'Sfunny thing, by golly, but the dang' critter got up all by hisself today. 'Pears to be gettin' better."

"One more thing, pardner. Were Tallant an' Dodge friends?"

The hostler shrugged a little. "No, I wouldn't call 'em exactly friends. Y'see, Tallant's hell to gamble, an', near as I can figger out, old man Dodge set him up in this here livery barn with a big loan. Les's been gamblin' pretty heavy, an' once I heard 'em cussin' at each other in the office. 'Course, I wasn't eavesdroppin', y'understand. . . ."

" 'Course not, I understand." If there was a tinge of amused sarcasm in the Kid's voice, the hostler didn't get it.

"Anyway, like I was sayin', they was hollerin' at one another an' Dodge tol' Les, if he didn't keep his word on the note, they'd have some trouble."

"How long was that before Dodge got killed?"

"Oh, hell, I don't rightly know. Six months maybe, maybe eight months." The old cowboy screwed up his face. "Say, you don't think Les Tallant killed the old man, do you? Hell, from what I heard around town, they was more'n one man in at the shootin'."

The Kid reached into his pocket and shrugged at the same time. He passed the hostler a gold piece and watched the avaricious glitter come into the whiskey-rheumy eyes. "No. I don't allow Tallant did the killin' by himself. *¿Quién sabe?* Who knows who did it, or how many there were?" He thanked the hostler, and ducked back out of town.

The Kid had the thing pretty well worked out in his mind before he moved out of his lair among the juniper hills. It wasn't exactly clear to him, yet, what it was all about, but somehow he felt that he'd stumbled onto a short-cut to the killers. He leisurely saddled up the big black, hummed in the late afternoon, checked his gun and belt loops, swung aboard, and rode carefully out over the moonlit range. The night was balmy, like there might be summer rain in the offing, and the full, mellow light of the heavens covered the land with its mantle of eerie, soft, and mysterious light.

The Kid rode for several hours before he came to the knoll where he'd watched the D-Back-To-Back ranch yard the day of his gunfight with Dugan and Beale. Like a ghostly silhouette, the Kid sat in a pensive mood, overlooking the ranch below. The buildings were dark. The Kid dismounted, shucked his spurs, hobbled his horse, and began the descent to the ranch yard below. He knew the way, this time, and, by the time the back of the house loomed up before him, he had taken only a fraction of the time he had used on his first abortive visit to Toma Dodge.

The Kid tried the window, found it not only unlocked, but easier to slide up than it had been before. A tiny tinkling of warning rang far back in the dim recesses of his mind but he shrugged them away. He was inside the room, flattened against the wall, hand hovering over his .45, listening, when the little warning buzzed again. This time, concentrating on the darkness as he was, the warning was limned sharply in his mind. He stood motionlessly and listened. Somewhere in the house he could hear voices. Men's voices. A full awareness of his position swept over him in an instant and he hesitated briefly, looking wonderingly at the opened window. The voices came again, dim and distant and incomprehensible, but unmistakable. He turned his back on the route of escape and began a sidling, stealthy advance across the room.

The Kid's eyes were accustomed to the gloom by the time he had been in the Dodge house for ten minutes. Still, he felt his way along the wall, careful not to bump into anything. He found a long, cool corridor and went down it. The voices were clearer now and suddenly he heard the voice of Toma Dodge. The words weren't hard to understand and they sent a chill over the Kid.

"No. You're both wrong. He told me about the two bullet holes, and I saw them for myself."

A masculine voice interrupted. "I told you we should've finished off the damned horse."

Another voice, garrulous and sullen, answered: "All right, I was wrong. As soon as she signs the deed, we'll go back an' kill the damn' critter."

The first voice answered swiftly and there was the sound of a man rising from his chair. "Come on, Toma, we ain't got all night. Sign it an' nothin'll happen to you."

"And if I don't?"

There was an unpleasant silence that the Kid felt and understood. He let his hand rest caressingly on his gun butt.

"An' if you don't, you'll get what your old man got."

"You'd do that to a woman?" Her voice was high and incredulous.

Apparently the man nodded because Toma's voice came again, softly, as though a dismal apathy had swept over her. "You'll never be able to get away with it."

"Let us worry about that, Toma. You jus' sign the deed."

The Vermilion Kid was as tense as a coiled spring. He was prepared to go into violent action on an instant's notice. There was a long silence from the other room, then the Kid relaxed and turned away as he heard one of the men sigh and speak: "That's more like it, Toma. Now you're as safe as can be."

The Kid was lowering himself out of the window when Toma answered, but he couldn't hear her reply. He thought: *You're not safe, though, Jeff Beale. You've made the greatest mistake of your life.*

The Kid ran in a crouched, zigzag course back to his waiting horse. He slipped off the hobbles after pulling on the split-ear bridle, mounted in a flying leap of frantic hoof beats, and rode down the night like a wraith of doom, thundering along the trackless range, a faint, ghostly figure bent on an act of justice that would thwart, if timely enough, the evil plans of two ruthless murderers.

Holbrook was noisy in a desultory sort of way. It was a weekday night and the revelers that inundated the town on Saturday night were mostly asleep in the bunkhouses across the cattle country. Even so, however, there was enough noise to mute down the thundering approach of hoof beats. The raucous screech of a protesting piano, accompanied by a nasal tenor, frequently drowned out by the laughter, shouts, and curses of the saloon clientele, ignored the narrow-eyed rider who swung down inside Tallant's livery barn, tense and with probing, hard eyes of smoke-gray.

Disturbed in his secret libations, the bleary-eyed hostler came grumblingly out of a dark stall where a mound of unclean hay served as couch, bed, and bar. Looking up when he was close enough to discern the night traveler, the hostler gave a small start and shook his head. "Too late, pardner, too late."

The Kid stepped forward. "What d'ya mean, too late?"

"Jus' what I said. Sheriff Dugan's got a warrant out for you. Dead or alive. You're a goner."

The Kid appraised the man. He wondered if the man was too drunk to trust. "Pardner, just how drunk are you, anyway?"

The hostler's face got a sullen smear of color in his cheeks and his eyes were surly. "Not so drunk that I don't know a thing or two. Why?"

The Kid jumped in whole hog. He had no other choice. "Because, pardner, a man's life depends on you tonight."

"That so? Whose?"

"Mine, *amigo*, mine."

The hostler looked owlishly at the Kid and a stray strand of his old-time decency flared up in a quick, final effort to assert itself. The man's voice was suddenly very steady and sincere and his jaw shot out a little. "All right, pardner, start at the beginnin'."

"Tallant an' Jeff Beale are on their way here to kill Dodge's horse tonight."

The hostler made a forlorn little clucking sound in his throat. "An' the poor critter's on the mend, too. Damned if I don't believe he's goin' to pull through, after all."

The Kid let the interruption run its course. "Listen, pardner, I want you to hide my horse in one of those back stalls. Don't unsaddle or unbridle him. Jus' close the door to the stall and fork him a little hay so's he'll be quiet."

"That all?"

"No. I want you to take a note over to Sheriff Dugan an' then stay out of the barn until the shootin's over. Understand?"

"I reckon. Where's the note?"

"Take care of my horse an' I'll write it."

The hostler nodded, took the Kid's reins, and led the black horse off into the dark recesses of the old barn. The Kid tore a handbill of himself off the barn wall, scrabbled a stubby pencil out of a shirt pocket, and wrote frowningly until the sot returned. He folded the coarse paper and handed it to his accomplice. "Pardner, here's where you've got the whiphand. If you double-cross me an' hand that there paper to Tallant, Beale . . . or anyone besides the sheriff . . . I'm done for."

The old cowboy pulled himself up in his filthy rags and his watery brown eyes were stern. "I'm a lot of things, *compadre*, but a bushwhacker ain't one of 'em."

The Kid nodded softly. "I believe you, pardner. On your way."

The hostler had disappeared down the plank sidewalk and the

Kid had hidden himself behind some loose planks in the gloom of the building, before the sound of horses came to him over the sounds of revelry. He watched, motionless, as Beale and Tallant swung down, tied their horses in tie stalls, loosened their *cinchas,* and looked at one another.

Beale spoke first. "Went off like clockwork."

"Yeah. All we got to do is make two more killings. Blast the damned horse, then go back an' get the girl, an' the whole shootin' match is ours."

Tallant nodded. "Yeah. It come off better'n I expected. Two more killin's an' the whole country'll be after the Vermilion Kid with orders from Dugan to shoot on sight. Hell, that dang' would-be owlhooter'll never get close enough to anybody to convince 'em he ain't guilty."

"Yeah, but what about the horse?"

Tallant rubbed his hands together. "That's the easiest part. We kill him, drag him off out on the range behind town, an' the coyotes'll have him torn to pieces in twenty-four hours. Nobody'll ever see them two holes again."

Beale swore gruffly. "Yeah. But if it hadn't been for that damned Kid, nobody'd ever've noticed there was two holes to start with."

Tallant laughed smoothly. "Don't make no difference now. Come on, let's go in the office an' have a drink afore we finish off the horse."

Beale nodded heavily. "Sure, we'll be ridin' again, back to the D-Back-To-Back for Toma before this night's work is done, so I reckon we'll need the lift, eh?"

Tallant didn't answer and the Kid could barely make out his outline and hear the soft music of his spurs as the two men went into the cubbyhole office, lit a lamp that cast a rich, yellowish light, and drank deeply from a brown bottle Tallant got out of the safe.

The Kid's fury was murderously cold. That Beale and Tallant intended to shoot down Toma Dodge was almost overpowering him.

Jeff Beale came out of the office first. He hesitated at the door, waiting for Tallant to lock up the whiskey bottle in the safe again. Tallant's garrulous voice came to him: "If I don't lock up the whiskey in the safe, that damned booze hound I got for a hostler'll steal it all."

Beale didn't answer. He was studying the mellow moonlight inside the barn. He finally got impatient: "Come on, dammit."

Tallant slammed the safe door, spun the dial, and hurried out of the office. The two men walked down the long, wide corridor toward the stall of the wounded horse. Tallant walked with the sure steps of a man to whom the darkness posed no deterrent, but Beale swore dourly to himself and made slower time. Tallant stopped at a stall directly across from the Kid's hide-out and waited for Beale to come up.

"He's in here."

"If you shoot him, it'll make too much noise."

"Ain't goin' to shoot him. Goin' to knock him over the poll with my gun barrel."

Tallant swung open the door as Beale came up. "Lead him out here to the alley. He'll be too hard to snake outen the stall when he's dead."

"Right." Tallant put a shank to the horse's halter and led the weak, stumbling animal through the doorway. Beale swore savagely at the animal's slow progress and kicked out viciously, striking the horse in the stomach. The animal flinched and grunted with pain. The Kid's eyes flamed in the darkness. Tallant turned the big bay so that he faced the rear door of the barn, drew his gun, tossed a quick look at Beale, who nodded indifferently, his evil face twisted into a cruel grin of anticipation, then all hell broke loose.

67

There was a thunderous, magnified echo from inside the barn and Tallant's six-gun went flipping out of his hand as though plucked from his startled fingers by an invisible hand. The bay horse jumped frantically and lurched out of the barn's rear doorway. Beale ripped out an obscene oath and threw himself sideways to the ground. Les Tallant stood for a full ten seconds, incredulous and unbelieving, then he leaned quickly backward into the recently vacated stall and ran his hand, like the striking tongue of a rattler, under his coat and came up with a big-bore little Derringer.

Jeff Beale had seen the mushroom of flame from the Kid's gun and fired as soon as he hit the ground, then rolled away, waiting for the answering shot that never came. Beale's breathing sounded as loud as the puffing of a locomotive in his own ears. He strained his eyes into the gloom for a target, saw none, listened acutely, heard nothing, threw two more snap shots toward where the flame had been, and waited. He began to hope that his first shot had found the hidden gunman, and, as the seconds ticked by, he felt certain that the hidden assassin had been knocked off with his first shot.

"Les?"

For a long moment Tallant didn't answer, then, seeing that no exploratory shots came toward Beale's voice, he answered: "Yes?"

"Think I got him with the first shot?"

Another pause, then Tallant's voice, cautious and soft, came back: "Who is it?"

Beale's voice was almost normal now. He was certain the unseen gunman had been killed outright. "Hell, how should I know? I can't see in the dark like no damned cat."

Tallant made out the rising form of his partner, coming erect off the floor of the barn. "Be careful, Jeff. He might be playin' 'possum."

"I'll damned soon find out."

Walking slowly forward, Jeff Beale was crouched almost double, his gun held out in front of him, when the second shot came out of the darkness. Tallant saw the flash out of the corner of his eye and heard the roar even as he fired and saw Beale go down in a cursing heap. He fired again and again, then suddenly the little Derringer was empty. The acrid smell of gunsmoke was thick in the air and some of the stalled horses were snorting wildly in fear.

Tallant was panicky. He was unarmed now, and Beale was hit. A thought flashed across his mind and he darted toward the fallen man, jerked the .45 from his fingers, and ran zigzag through the barn toward the tie stalls and his snorting, wild-eyed horse as Jeff Beale called after him. Once, Tallant whirled, aimed carefully, and pulled the trigger. Beale abruptly stopped his swearing, jerked spasmodically against the violence of his suddenly short-circuited nervous system, and went limp, twitching dully over the freshly raked, hard-packed earth of the livery barn floor.

Seeing Tallant on the verge of escape, the Vermilion Kid leaped stiffly from his hiding place, ran to the middle of the alleyway, unmindful of the clear outline of the moonlight behind him that silhouetted him into a perfect target. "Don't move, Tallant. Get away from that horse's head."

Tallant was obsessed with an insane urge to flee. He was beyond reason. He whirled, threw up his gun, and fired. The Kid staggered backward, went down to one knee, and his head drooped. Only one thing made it possible for him to force his mind and muscles to work, the certain knowledge that Tallant was on his way to kill Toma Dodge.

He brought up his right arm. The gun weighed 100 pounds. Its barrel weaved unsteadily, and, as the Kid squeezed the trigger, he saw a vague, shapeless figure leap out of the shadows and attach itself to the bridle of the horse that Tallant had just swung upon. He saw, too, the quick, descending arc as Tallant's gun came down, and the orange tongue of flame when he fired. The ragged figure fell suddenly to earth. The Kid squeezed the trigger and saw Tallant straighten in the saddle. The blasting roar of another gunshot split the night, and the Kid sank down.

When the Vermilion Kid opened his eyes, he was looking into the hard, relentless face of Sheriff Dugan. His eyes wandered from Dugan's flinty features to the surrounding walls and ceiling. He had never been in the sheriff's office before, but he knew he was lying on a makeshift cot behind Dugan's untidy desk. He swung his eyes back to Dugan. "You got the note?"

Dugan nodded dumbly.

"Where's the bay horse? Seems a shame that a horse as gutsy as he is damned near got killed."

Dugan's eyes clouded for just an instant, then the film of hardness settled into place once more. "He's goin' to be all right. Some of the D-Back-To-Back riders led him out to the ranch. The old boy's lookin' a little better all the time. He's goin' to make it, all right." The sheriff's voice drifted off and faded out altogether.

The Kid nodded slightly. "What happened after I took my *siesta?*"

"Nothin' much. Tallant was fixin' to ride out when old Bob, the hostler, jumped him an' tried to pull him off his horse. He shot the old boy dead."

There was an awkward moment of silence as each man, in his own way, said a rough, embarrassed prayer for the drunkard. Dugan cleared his throat loudly. "After I got your note about Tallant and Beale wantin' to kill the horse, I loped down there an' got there just as Bob made his play. I could dimly see you kneelin' in the back o' the barn, near Beale's body. Les Tallant threw down on me, an' I shot him out o' the saddle. That's all there was to it."

The Kid's eyes strayed around the room again and came up suddenly, wide and incredulous. Toma Dodge was sitting, small and fragile, white-faced and big-eyed, near Dugan's desk. The Kid swallowed a couple of times quickly and felt the blood rushing into his face. Dugan cast a quick, furtive look at the two of them, arose, coughed, and ambled toward the door. When he was at the opening, he turned slowly.

"Take it easy, Kid. You got a bad notch in the side. Three inches more to the left and you'd've been makin' the long march with Beale." He let his eyes wander aimlessly to Toma, small and slightly flushed, in the old cane-backed chair. "Sorta look after him for a spell, will you, Toma? I got to go . . . uh . . . uptown for a few minutes." Dugan closed the door softly behind him and strolled slowly down the roadway toward the silent, gloomy maw of the livery barn.

"Miss Dodge, I. . . ."

"Toma."

"Uh, yeah. Toma, I reckon we figured this thing out pretty well, at that, didn't we?"

"Yes." Her lips quivered for a moment and the reserve melted away. "Oh, Kid I'm so sorry I misjudged you." She left the chair and went up closer to the improvised cot. The Kid smiled up at her and the faint little wistful smile tugged at the corners of his mouth.

" 'To a man from a cesspool, the gutter is heaven,'" he quoted softly.

There were misty tears in her violet eyes. She bent down swiftly and her warm, moist lips clung to his for a tremulous moment, then she arose and turned away. He recovered from his startled attitude as she reached the door.

"Toma?"

"Yes?"

"Did you do that because I'm hurt an' you feel sorry for me?"

"No."

His head came off the pallet. "Then I'll be ridin' out to the D-Back-To-Back in a day or two."

She went through the door with a high blush on her face, but there was also a demure flash of affection in her eyes and the answer came back softly to the Kid. "I'll be waiting for you."

★ ★ ★ ★ ★

# The Plains of Laramie

★ ★ ★ ★ ★

# I

Laramie lay in its breathless heat and the plains lay brown to their distant ending against blue-glazed mountains. Frank Travis had crossed the Laramie Plains, that immense and seemingly endless stretch of flatland running from east to west and from the mountains southward down into Colorado, buckling near Tie Siding and Virginia Dale into parks and forests and rocky breaks.

His crossing had one purpose. It had to have; no one in their right mind crossed the Laramie Plains in full summer unless they had a sound reason for doing so. At times that searing scorch was unbearable even to the Indians who'd been on the plains for thousands of years and should have therefore been inured to summer heat.

The heat bothered him, but Frank was a native Arizonan. He'd lived among some of the most adroit people in the world where heat was concerned—Mexicans. He'd learned as a little boy how to relax, how to avoid unnecessary exertion and movement, how to keep a little round stone in his mouth to promote saliva flow, and, finally, he had learned the main secret of living with heat—think about it as little as possible and never be angry about it.

That was the way he appeared over the Laramie Plains, slouched in the saddle, philosophically accepting discomfort, patiently awaiting dusk, the earth's ultimate cooling, and his arrival in the far-ahead, shimmering village of Laramie.

That was the way the posse found him as they swept up over the shimmering horizon, spied that solitary figure passing steadily along, and rushed at him all in a body, thirty of them, every one a hard man, every one of them armed with a six-gun and carbine, each sun-layered face bleak with cold wrath and oily with perspiration.

Frank saw them coming. He considered their numbers and also the bunched-up way they were riding, and initially these things did not disturb him. But when he saw evil sun glare reflecting off armament, saw the lead horseman swing abruptly toward him and boot his beast over into a long lope, Frank felt sudden concern. He had no idea this was a posse under Sheriff Ken Wheaton; he saw no badge at that distance.

But Arizona or Wyoming, or almost anywhere else for that matter west of the Missouri River, when a traveler saw a hard-riding mob of heavily armed horsemen coming purposefully and grimly toward him, he did not ordinarily accept those odds with equanimity, and neither did Frank Travis. He had come a long way, his horse was heat-wilted, and to race in that dancing heat was suicidal, but Frank Travis accepted what he considered the inevitability of this, rowelled his astonished horse, and it plunged wildly around and went in headlong flight over the westward plain.

As soon as Frank turned tail and raced away, those oncoming riders raised a high yell. Two of them fired guns but the distance was too great. Still, those shots confirmed Frank in the suspicion that he was being pursued by one of the numerous outlaw gangs for which this north country was notorious.

He didn't like doing it, but he hooked his horse again. The animal was a thoroughbred, Frank's pride and his joy. His brother had given it to him two years earlier on Frank's twenty-first birthday. A fast horse even more than a fast gun was a man's life insurance in the West. Frank's beast responded to this second spurring with an additional burst of speed. He was spending his reserve strength rapidly now, but his heart was strong. He swept along in a belly-down run for two scalding miles, then began to slacken, great lungs working like bellows, red inside nostril lining extended its full limit as he sucked avidly for more of the hot, thin, high country air.

Frank drew him in a little. He twisted to look back. All but three of his pursuers had fallen out of the race. Those three, wise in the ways of the summertime plains, were not closing the distance between themselves and Frank; they were instead loping slowly along keeping him well in sight. This was an old Indian trick. If a pursuer could not run down his prey, he walked it down, by persistence, by going without food or water or rest. The pursuer would doggedly keep at it until he overtook his enemy.

Frank recognized what those men were doing. He drew the thoroughbred down to an alternating slow lope and fast walk. Sweat darkened the horse's satiny hide to a rich glossy wetness. He rolled the cricket and fought the bit wishing to run again; Frank held him down.

Those three grim horsemen far back kept at it. As the sun glided off center, they loped, then walked. They sometimes stole a march on Frank by trotting. But this was a gait few Westerners ever used and Frank's pursuers did not trot often, which in the end prolonged the conclusion of this silent, bizarre pursuit.

From time to time Frank saw a few of those other riders come up from farther back, but generally these other posse men had been outdistanced. Some, in fact, had abandoned the chase in discomfort and disgust and had put about, heading for the village that was no longer in sight.

He did not know this country at all, yet he was instinctively and acutely conscious that unless and until he could get off the Laramie Plains, could get into some shielding hills or into a forest of trees, those moving dark shapes far back there would always have him in sight, and probably, in the end, because they knew where water was in this sere world and Frank did not, they would overtake him.

The pivot of survival for Frank Travis was his thoroughbred horse. This handsome big blood bay animal may have lacked the seasoned toughness of those coarser beasts far back; he may have come a greater distance under the blasting summertime sun, but he had the speed to outdistance his pursuers completely. It was this that Frank was relying upon; if he had to, he could use the swiftness of his mount to escape. But if he did this, he very well knew, he would probably kill the thoroughbred or at the least break its wind. Either of those things would put Frank at the complete mercy of his pursuers, and he had no doubt at all about the limit of that kind of mercy. Road agents were notorious for killing anyone they robbed, in order that no living witnesses ever identified them.

The race continued. Frank kept just beyond Winchester range, and his pursuers plodded after him as stubbornly persistent as men could be. Sun glare diminished; a reddish brightness lay rustily over the countryside. The race became now a test of endurance. Men and animals moved mechanically, eyes inflamed, throats tortured, and muscles jerky with dehydration, with fatigue. The end could not be postponed much longer. Frank gradually accepted this nearing finality and assumed that those three men behind him, all that remained in sight now of the original thirty, also understood this.

He began to view those onward mountains without hope; they were still retreating, still miles away. Northward it was the same, Laramie Plains all the way to other blue-blurred forested lifts and peaks. That flat, summer-hard land ran on like an oily sea frozen in motion. Southward, too, there was nothing, no trees, no rocks, not even erosion gullies as far as Frank could see.

His blood bay horse began to lag.

Far back those three grim pursuers were still there. One of them was dropping back from the others, his horse also nearly finished. The other two, however, were still coming on. They no longer loped but they alternately walked and trotted. Beyond them there was nothing to be seen of their companions. A filmy heat haze back there obscured the horizon, made it shimmer and fade out, firm up, then fade again.

The day was close to ending. Dusk would come, and after that night, but full darkness would not descend until near nine o'clock. Frank knew this and was discouraged from believing nightfall could succor him. He had only one hope of escape, and that was the thoroughbred horse under him.

Time flowed. Frank favored his mount as much as possible, but obviously the hours-long chase had drained away the thoroughbred's last reserves of strength.

Only two pursuers were now in sight far back. Frank was considering them, balancing in his mind the odds of survival. He was sitting, twisted in the saddle, both booted feet lightly touching his Visalia stirrups. He was not looking ahead at all and therefore did not know he and his horse had entered the honeycombed ground area of a prairie dog village until, without even a grunt, his animal stepped upon weakened ground, broke through up to his fetlocks, and fell heavily. Frank was shot ahead. He landed hard and lay a second without moving, without immediately comprehending what had happened. He rolled over, got up onto one knee, and saw his horse struggling upright with one front leg held clear as though injured or broken. One glance at the caved-in earth, the myriad holes roundabout, explained what had happened. He stood up, mechanically struck at the gray dust, then went over where the thoroughbred was standing head down, eyes glazed, that injured foreleg held up.

"This is where we part company," he told the horse as though speaking to another man. "You did your best. Except for the prairie dog village we'd have made it, old-timer." He ran a gentle hand over the animal's quivering shoulder, drew his carbine, looked back where those two remaining pursuers were coming together, were stopping to speak, and also draw forth their saddle guns, then he did what he could for the horse. He tugged loose the *cincha,* the flank rigging, dropped the saddle at his feet, cast down the sweat-stiff blanket, removed the bridle, and gently struck the horse over the rump.

"Move off," he said. "No point in you getting it, too."

The horse responded with several awkward hops, still favoring that sprained ankle. Frank caught up the saddle, walked northward a little distance, threw it down, and got down flat behind it with his Winchester. He did not have a good defense; against one man it might have been adequate but not against two men. Two men could do what had to be done easily, one in front, one behind.

He levered up a load, placed the carbine over his saddle seat, and waited. He was thirst-tortured; each time his eyes moved, it felt as though he had granules of sand under his eyelids. That blood-red sun, which was falling away in the west, burned against his back, his shoulders, his saddle-molded legs.

Those two unrelenting horsemen began their slow advance. Behind them the third rider was coming up again. None of those three men hurried; even if their horses had been capable of hurry, there was no longer any need for it.

They halted again just beyond carbine range; they turned to wave the third man forward. Some little time passed before the three of them were all together, but even then they evidenced no eagerness. They sat out there in that reddening immensity of dead land like some bizarre variety of carrion eater, looking ahead where Frank Travis lay forted up behind his saddle, speaking quietly among themselves, planning what they would do and how they must do it. Once or twice they looked back for the balance of the riders who had been with them; this was their only indication of uneasiness.

Frank's body oozed sweat where scorched earth touched him. He ran a soiled sleeve over his face, let the arm fall upon the saddlebags behind his saddle cantle, and followed out the movement of that arm. He gazed at those saddlebags with irony; he ran his free hand over their scuffed and bulging exterior, thinking back down the years for this little quiet time as men sometimes do when the scent of death is close and unmistakable.

He looked around for the thoroughbred, saw him hobbling toward a clump of buffalo grass with that swollen foreleg six inches off the ground, and called softly: "Thanks and good luck, pardner."

A thin, fluting call rode the westward air from out where those three horsemen were. Frank swung his wandering thoughts, his full attention back to them. They were breaking up as he'd known they would. One was coming straight at him; another was riding widely around to come in upon him from behind. The third man was swinging wide, too, in the opposite direction; he would come in from that side.

Frank swore under his breath saying—"Get it over with."— and called those three strangers harsh names.

He watched to see which rider would come into range first. But these were canny plainsmen; they remained just out of bullet reach as they circled and tacked and angled onward. They seemed to know almost to the foot just how far Frank's carbine would reach. When they were finally in position, the man who was to strike from Frank's rear dismounted, drew his carbine, and dropped down to one knee. He made a poor target in that failing red light low upon the cooling earth, but Frank twisted and fired at him just the same.

At once all three enemies fired back. Frank whipped around as the northward man dashed suddenly ahead Indian-like and threw himself flat to blend with the puddling shadows. Frank would have fired at this man but he had no time. The southward man got off a shot, then the rearward man also fired. The northward man lunged upright and raced ahead again. This time Frank fired. Dust spurted a yard ahead of his racing foeman. The running man dropped like a stone. He did not return Frank's shot. He began snake-crawling forward, using his punched-down carbine butt for balance and purchase. Of the three he was closest. Frank swung to concentrate upon this man. He levered and fired, saw dust spurt, saw that crawling man frantically change course, and fired again.

Behind him a slamming explosion showed that another enemy was also running in now. That bullet pierced Frank's saddle skirt. From southward came another near miss; this one struck through the *rosadero*.

Frank's vision cleared and his tormenting thirst was entirely forgotten. He had only a few moments left. He ignored those near misses to put his whole attention upon that northward crawling man. He came up off the ground to one knee. A slug struck leather beside him, tore into saddle swells, and violently upturned the saddle. Frank ignored it. He tracked that northward enemy, caught him in his sights, drew him down the barrel, and fired. The crawling man jerked up off the ground like a broken doll; he flung away his Winchester; he fell back and flopped frantically with diminishing motions until he lay quite still.

Frank was turning away, was levering up another bullet. He did not hear the gunfire; he only felt a sudden burst of heat inside him, then he tumbled into a suffocating black and spiraling void.

# II

Laramie had a grand funeral for Sheriff Ken Wheaton, killed by the unknown outlaw with all that money in his saddlebags who had been also killed by Ken Wheaton's two posse men westward on the Laramie Plains.

The other dead man of that encounter was brought to town under a soiled old canvas in the back of Johnny Fleharty's buckboard. His name, according to the one letter found upon him, was Frank Travis. Beyond that, there was nothing among his effects to tell the people of Laramie who he was—except that $9,000 in gold in his saddlebags—and that was shy $3,000 of the amount stolen from the Laramie Express Company the day Sheriff Wheaton and his posse had ridden northward seeking the bandit who had robbed the express office in broad daylight.

There was considerable speculation over what this outlaw Travis could have done with the missing $3,000. According to the men of Wheaton's posse, they had encountered Travis six miles out. He was, they related, riding along as though he hadn't a worry in the world, and he'd been quite alone.

"If he didn't pass it to a pardner," Johnny Fleharty asked across his bar at the Great Northern Saloon, "what *did* he do with it?"

"Buried it most likely," replied Ace McElhaney, gazing moodily into his partially empty beer glass. "Don't ask me why he buried it, though."

"So he'd have a nest egg," spoke up Charles Swindin of the Lincoln Ranch, east of town. "They do that sometimes, I've heard. Cache loot here an' there so's, when they're broke, they got something to dig up an' use as a stake."

Johnny Fleharty turned this over in his mind for a moment, drew two more glasses of beer, set one each in front of Charley and Ace, then nodded tacit agreement. "Had to be something like that. He sure didn't throw it away or we'd have found it out there."

Ace looked around at Swindin. "Say, how's that blood bay comin' along?"

"Comin' along fine. It was a bad sprain, but he'll be good as new in another month or two."

Ace returned to considering his beer. "I'd have bet money that leg was broke. The critter looked like he was done for, too. How's his wind?"

"It's sound," said Charley. "All that big horse needs is lots of rest and he's goin' to get it." Charley lifted his glass, drained it, and put it down in its little pool of stickiness again. "Lew swears that horse is a thoroughbred."

"Lew knows horses," stated Fleharty, then brightened. "Lew's in town today. Did you fellers know that?"

Both Swindin and McElhaney shook their heads.

"He's after the town council to appoint Hubbell Wheaton to his brother's job as sheriff."

This brought no immediate response from either of his listeners, but after a while Ace said: "Hub's a good man. He'd do all right."

Swindin agreed indifferently with this. "Yeah, anyway I don't expect any other robber'll be anxious to come bustin' in here after what happened to Travis."

"Nobody ever told me," said Fleharty, looking from Swindin to McElhaney. "Just which one of you fired the shot that got him, out there?"

Ace straightened up off the bar. He was a big man with a coarse face, heavy shoulders, and a slash of a mouth. He ran pale eyes over the quiet room where card players whiled away the afternoon hours content to do anything that kept them in out of the sun, and he said: "Who knows, Johnny? He took two slugs. Doc Spence says either of 'em would have killed him."

Lank Charley nodded over this, pushed his empty glass away, ran a sleeve across chapped lips, and mightily yawned. "I got the blood bay," he said. "I figure I got well paid."

Big Ace put his heavy-lidded look around. "You'll likely be the only feller who'll benefit from all that damned ridin' too, Charley, because there don't seem to be no Wanted poster out for that Travis."

Fleharty said: "You'll get your regular pay for bein' a posse man, Ace."

"Yeah. A lousy dollar, an' I liked to rode my horse to death. Hell, Johnny, it was a hundred and twenty out there in that sunshine." McElhaney drew upright. "I'll give you fifty bucks for the blood bay horse, Charley," he said.

Swindin shook his head. "I got plans for that animal. When he's sound again, I'm goin' to find out just how fast he can run. Then I'll maybe take him 'round to the fairs and make a killin' with him."

"He can run all right," stated Ace. "I'll be damned if he can't. You recollect how he left us all behind like we was tied to trees when Travis first broke away? Well, you let me know when you're goin' to run him . . . I want to be there an' see that."

Charley Swindin smiled, dabbed at sweat with a crusted bandanna, and moved off. "See you fellers later," he said, crossed to the spindle doors, and passed beyond sight out into the sun-blasted roadway.

"I ought to be goin' along, too," McElhaney said, looking out into the bitter-bright roadway. "Damn but it's hot."

"Have another beer."

"Naw, makes a feller sweat too much in weather like this.

Besides, I get kind o' drowsy when I drink in hot weather."
McElhaney, though, made no move away from the coolness of
the bar; in fact, he hooked both elbows over it and leaned there,
his broad back to Johnny Fleharty, his hat far back, and rumpled
hair low across his forehead.

Everyone in that room was drained of energy. Even the card
players seemed motivated by an inertia that went deeply into
each man. Their reflexes were slow, their words slurred, and
every face in the saloon was stolidly heavy and stupid-appearing.

"Johnny," said McElhaney without turning, "I keep wonderin'
about that three thousand dollars. He didn't throw it away an'
he didn't drop it. It wasn't in the saddlebags when the money
was counted . . . so where is it?"

Fleharty swiped the bar top with a smelly cloth. "He hid it
like Charley said. He had to hide it, otherwise it'd have showed
up by now. Unless. . . ."

"Unless what?"

"Nothin'."

McElhaney turned. He stared at Fleharty. "Come on, out
with it," he said. "If we could find it, there'd be fifteen hundred
apiece."

"Well, I was just thinkin' that, after Travis was killed, maybe
somebody took three thousand outen his saddlebags. Or maybe
he was carryin' that much in his pockets."

Ace continued his staring. "Johnny," he said softly, "you know
damned well who was there when Travis was shot. Me 'n' Charley Swindin. Wheaton was dead, an' the others hadn't come up
yet. Now what you're sayin' is that. . . ."

"No. No, I'm not sayin' any such a thing, Ace. It wouldn't
have had to be either you or Charley, anyway. The others came
up, too."

"Not for a half hour," muttered McElhaney. "An' even after

they did, there wasn't a chance . . . too many fellers standin' around there."

"Well, didn't someone search Travis?"

"Sure. Lew Morgan did, an' Hub Wheaton was kneelin' right beside him. That's when they found all that gold in the saddlebags. But, hell, by then no one could've. . . ."

"You mean you an' Charley didn't even look in the saddlebags, Ace?"

"No. Why should we? We had no idea there'd be gold in there, Johnny. It was hotter than the hubs of hell. We was both about played out, and there was Travis, lyin' all sprawled out in front of us. Who'd think to search a man or look into his saddlebags at a time like that?"

Johnny finished with the sour bar rag. He faintly smiled with his bright blue eyes. "I would," he said quietly. "I've seen dead men before. They don't bother me a bit. Besides, whatever they got, they're not goin' to take with 'em. That's how I look at it, Ace."

McElhaney kept staring at Fleharty. He seemed annoyed. "It's done now an' over with," he growled. "Charley got the blood bay horse. The rest of us that was in the damned posse'll get our dollar a day from Wheaton's cash fund like always . . . and the sheriff's coolin' out under six feet of sod."

Fleharty cocked his head at McElhaney. "What about the three thousand?" he asked.

McElhaney leaned farther over the bar. He cupped his bristly chin in one big hand and stared thoughtfully at the painting of a voluptuous reclining nude woman hanging over Fleharty's backbar.

"He didn't spend it. He didn't drop it. He didn't have it on him, at least as far as I know he didn't. So . . . it's got to be out there somewhere, an' that's all there is to it."

McElhaney drew upright again. He scowled at Fleharty. "But

where? Dammit, the Laramie Plains are bigger'n kingdom come."

"No rocks," murmured Johnny. "No caves or trees or mine-shafts out there."

Ace said irritably: "I know what there *ain't,* damn it. Tell me what there *is.*"

Johnny slyly smiled. "Three thousand dollars," he crooned. "Three thousand gold dollars hidden somewhere, sure as God made green apples."

Ace said a harsh word in powerful disgust, turned, and walked out of the saloon. He halted under Fleharty's wooden roadside awning and puckered his eyes against sun smash. Across the road burly Lewis Morgan and lanky, youthful, and tough-looking Hubbell Wheaton were in deep conversation. McEl-haney watched them. Morgan was speaking with, for him, unaccustomed vehemence. He was even occasionally gesturing with his hands, something Ace had never before known him to do.

Lew Morgan owned the Lincoln Ranch of which Charley Swindin was foreman. Lew, at fifty-five, was in better physical shape than many men half his age. He had iron-gray hair above a sun-darkened face. He was wealthy and powerful and bull-like.

Hubbell Wheaton, the dead sheriff's younger brother, was in appearance at least the opposite of Lew Morgan. Hub was well over six feet in height; he was that leaned-down sinewy type of man whose endurance was nearly limitless. Like the dead law-man, Hubbell's face was long and, viewed one way, gloomy. His eyes were very pale blue and his hair was like bleached straw. His general appearance was uncompromising and dour, but this was not entirely true because Hub Wheaton, while not a talkative man, was easy to know and in fact he had a quiet, forthright, even humorous disposition. But if little of this showed now, so soon after his brother's killing, it was understandable.

Ace McElhaney, who had worked with Hubbell Wheaton as a rider for the big cow outfits, felt envy at the way Lew Morgan was obviously treating Hub as his equal now. Ace was that kind of a man. He had his share of envy, and he also had a meanness of spirit that those who knew him well were also aware of. Particularly the riders who had been paired up with McElhaney on the roundups, for where two men eat, sleep, and work side-by-side for weeks at a time, all the little defects come out.

It made Ace antagonistic now, seeing rich Lew Morgan standing over there talking to Hub Wheaton like that, as though he wished for Wheaton's approval of something, as though he were pleading with Hub.

Ace stepped out into the roadway. As he walked forward, dust spurted underfoot and that malevolent afternoon sunlight bore down upon him. When he was close enough to be readily heard by those two conversing men, he brought up a hard, faint smile and called forward.

"You two figured where that other three thousand is yet?"

Morgan turned, hesitating in mid-sentence. Hubbell Wheaton's pale eyes lifted, ran over to McElhaney, and stayed there. Ace stopped at the plank walk's edge. He got the sudden feeling that his casual remark had struck like iron against flint with those two; they kept looking at him, making no effort to resume their conversation. Then Lew Morgan said rather briskly—"Well, think it over, Hub. I'll see you again."—and walked away.

Ace looked after Morgan; a faint blush of color came into his face. Morgan had not even nodded to him; he had simply turned and walked off.

Hubbell Wheaton saw that look and also the swift rise of a fiery antagonism in McElhaney's gaze. He said: "You could've said just about anything but what you did say, Ace. Morgan's about half believing what his niece said the day we brought Ken and Travis in."

Ace switched his smoky gaze to Hub. "Amy? What did she say?"

"That there was no three thousand dollars. That Travis only had nine thousand . . . and that it didn't come from the express office at all."

McElhaney got off a curse. "You believe that?" he demanded. "Dammit all, you come up after it was all over, Hub. You know how Travis put up a fight. Before that you saw how he tried like hell to escape from the posse."

"Amy's notion is that, when he saw thirty armed men bust out after him, he just naturally took fright and ran."

"Amy," snarled Ace. "What the hell would a woman know? Listen, how many common cowpunchers are ridin' around the Laramie Plains with nine thousand gold dollars in their saddle-bags?"

Wheaton, seeing the wrath in McElhaney's face, said: "Simmer down, Ace. *I* didn't say Travis wasn't the thief."

McElhaney teetered upon the plank walk's edge, saying fiercely: "Amy! Amy! That dog-goned spinster . . . why don't she just stick to her danged knittin'."

Hubbell fished in a pocket, brought forth a little badge, and held it in his palm. He used this to change the conversation. Ace glowered at the badge, his eyes still yeasty.

"I heard over at Johnny's place there was talk of givin' you Ken's job," he said, his voice losing some of its roughness. "I told 'em you'd make a good sheriff."

Hub considered the badge gravely and said: "Thanks, Ace. I aim to do my best." He pocketed the badge, looked across the road, and said: "Care for a drink?"

McElhaney lost some more of his indignation. "Why not?" he

said, reversed himself, and went with Hubbell Wheaton back across the road.

Down by the livery barn Lew Morgan saw those two hike out into the fierce sunlight where he was talking to Charley Swindin. He paused to watch their progress for a time, then he turned back to Charley again.

"Tell Amy I'll be late," he said. "I've got a little more business in town. And, Charley, pick up the mail before you head for the ranch."

# III

Amy Morgan was unmarried at twenty-four, which was almost unheard of on the frontier where men far outnumbered women. What made this even more incredible was that Amy Morgan was beautiful. She was slim and straight. Beneath heavy brows was the inquiring line of steel-gray eyes. She had skin the color of fresh butter and a long mouth that was composed. Her hair was red-auburn, the color of a winter sunset; it caught hot sunlight and threw it back in a coppery way. Her profile was cameo-like and head-on Amy had that indefinable, illusive quality that drew men to her in spite of themselves.

But Amy had not only a temper and a will of her own; she also had a mind to match. She'd had many suitors, but as she possessed that magnetic force that attracted men, she also had the very logical, skeptical, and analytical mind that could reduce them to nothing in conversation. Beautiful Amy Morgan was that bane of alluring women, a highly intelligent female in a man's world. That, in a breath, was why at twenty-four she was unmarried.

Amy was Lew Morgan's niece. Amy's dead father had been Lew's only brother. Amy's father had died four years earlier and she had come at Lew's invitation to live with him at Lincoln Ranch.

It was a good relationship between those two; Lew was a lifelong bachelor—he'd never had much use for women. Amy, the crispy efficient, seemingly cold-blooded but very beautiful woman, ran Lew's household and sometimes even ran Lincoln Ranch when Lew was absent. She never made a mistake and to Lew's astonishment—and delight—she reasoned like a man, so Lew treated her as an equal—something he'd never before done with a woman in his life.

Amy came down to breakfast the day following Hub Wheaton's appointment to fill out his dead brother's term as county sheriff looking cool and lovely. Lew, who had got in after midnight and was a little tired still, looked up at her as she swept forward toward the table, and smiled. Amy did not smile back. She sat down, unfolded her napkin, and waited for the cook to bring food. Lew's smile faded; he studied her expressionless face and grew uneasy. Lew Morgan was virile enough at fifty-five to respond to Amy's compelling allure, and at the same time old enough to be concerned with her thoughts and her opinions.

"What's bothering you?" he asked.

The cook came bearing their breakfast and Amy said nothing until he had retreated back into the kitchen. Then her head-on glance went to Lew and remained there as she spoke.

"I talked to Charley when he brought the mail last night. He told me about Hubbell Wheaton's appointment."

"Well, what's wrong with that?"

Amy called her uncle by his first name. That was his wish. The first time they'd met and she'd called him "Uncle Lew," it had stopped Lew Morgan cold. He'd been working so hard for thirty years that he'd lost track of time and that "Uncle Lew" had cruelly brought him up short, face to face with an inexorable march of time that left him breathless and stunned. Ever since then it had been just plain Lew and just plain Amy.

She said his name now, then also bluntly spoke her mind. "Lew, Ken Wheaton is dead. One death in that family is enough."

"What? What are you talking about?"

"I told you that the very fact that Travis did not have the full twelve thousand dollars which was stolen from the express company safe, although he was overtaken . . . and killed . . . before he could have spent, or even hidden any of it, meant that Travis was very possibly not the robber at all."

"All right, Amy," said Lew. "You told me that. What's it got to do with Ken and Hub Wheaton?"

"This, Lew. Charley told me about the letter found on young Travis."

Lew's cheeks darkened with color. He was becoming annoyed. His voice showed it, too, when he roughly said: "Quit beating around the bush, Amy. Young Travis had a letter on him. Dammit, what are you getting at?"

"Someone had to write that letter, Lew. Someone was close to Travis down in Arizona. Someone, probably the man who wrote that letter, will be coming to Laramie over Travis's killing." Amy paused to watch the gradual spread of understanding on her uncle's face. "If Frank Travis was not the express company robber . . . if he owned that nine thousand dollars in gold and the person who comes here knows that . . . then that person is also going to hear how Travis was shot to death without a chance by Sheriff Wheaton's posse . . . and to go just a little further, Lew . . . someone will very likely try to kill Charley and Ace McElhaney, the slayers of Travis, and probably Hub Wheaton as well."

Lew Morgan sat still for a half minute arranging all this in orderly sequence in his masculine mind—and came up with the identical sum total Amy had just given him in forceful words.

"I was in that posse, too," he ultimately said. "So was Ken. So was. . . ."

"Half the men in Laramie were in it according to Charley. And another thing, Lew . . . that blood bay horse. What right did Charley have to bring it here to the ranch? What right does he have keeping it at all?"

Lew had no answer, so he shrugged bull-like shoulders and reached for his coffee. "No one else wanted it. Everyone thought it had a broken leg." Lew sipped, put the cup down, and scowled. "If Charley left the critter out there, it would have died."

"I'm sure," said Amy dryly, "that's the only thought which motivated Charley . . . pity for an injured animal."

Lew squirmed. Amy had never approved of Charley Swindin, which was sometimes an issue between them. "Never mind the horse," he muttered, "and never mind Charley." He stood up. "I reckon I'll ride into town."

"For the letter?"

"Partly. To see it, anyway. Maybe the sender put a name on it. Otherwise, to talk this over with Hub. Hell, Amy, the only thought I had when I went before the town council for Hub was that he'd make a good sheriff, and it seemed right he should have the chance to finish Ken's term."

Amy's steely gaze softened toward her uncle. "I know," she said to him. "I understand, Lew, and I'm sorry if I poured cold water over your good deed. It's simply that, if trouble comes, Hub will be in the middle of it."

"You left something unsaid, Amy. You're thinking I put him there."

Amy answered this candidly, honestly, and quietly: "Yes." She stood up.

"Finish your breakfast," said Lew, turning away. "I'll be back directly." He took five steps, then swung around. "Maybe I'll bring Hub back for supper with me."

Those two exchanged a long look. Here was another issue between them—Amy's spinsterhood. Although Lew Morgan found the notion of marriage for himself anathema, he conversely thought Amy's singleness was some kind of a reflection upon the Morgan name.

"If you wish," said Amy in that chilly tone she used whenever she saw through her uncle and didn't approve. "I think I'll have a headache tonight and retire early, though."

Lincoln Ranch—so named because the original patent had been signed by President Abraham Lincoln—consisted of 17,000 acres of range, timber, water, and lush meadow. It lay southeast of Laramie and the Laramie-Cheyenne stage road crossed it for nearly six miles. A goodly portion of it lay upon the Laramie Plains, but not all of it. There were the places like Amy's little private dell up in the fragrant forest, where summertime heat lay, but where summertime sun never quite touched the spongy earth with its ancient carpeting of pine and fir needles. This was the place she frequently visited during hot days when there was nothing to hold her at the ranch. She rode to it an hour after her uncle left Lincoln Ranch for town, not particularly to escape the heat this time because as yet the day was young, the heat had not yet reached its zenith, but because she was troubled— had been troubled for several days now.

It was Amy's very strong suspicion that the tormenting heat, the rawness of summer-frayed tempers had led her uncle and those other men deliberately to kill an innocent man. She had listened to all that had been said about Frank Travis, had found most of it built upon the shifting sands of suspicion rather than upon the hard stone of logic, and now, riding to her private place, Amy was worried.

When she left her horse to go stand upon the bank of a little hurrying white-water creek that passed across her dell, to watch trout minnows scatter frantically at sight of her shadow upon the water, she had a premonition. It was very strong. It told her unmistakably that the passing of Frank Travis was not the ending but the beginning of events that were to touch the lives of everyone concerned with that killing.

# IV

It was not often that winds scoured the Laramie Plains in midsummer. During wintertime this was not so; the plains were notorious for their fiercely cold winter blows. Many a rider had sworn that regardless of how much clothing a man wore in wintertime, those frigid blasts knifed through them to freeze the flesh and chill the marrow.

Usually when a midsummer blow arrived upon the plains, it was a sign that one of those infrequent but awesome summer thunderstorms was approaching. This time, however, the sky was cloudless, brassy-pale, and the wind itself was hot. It curled leaves and wilted grass; it stung the flesh with abrasive dust and it burned the eyes with its dry heat. It was a very poor welcome for a stranger in the land such as Parker Travis, because it left him with a forming opinion that was half resentment and half dislike.

Parker Travis rode a long-legged seal-brown horse with sloping shoulders, a long barrel, and powerful rear quarters. He rode lightly for a big man, proving himself to be a horseman instead of a rider, the kind of man who never for a moment forgot the animal under him, its welfare, and its changing moods. He passed along with his collar turned up, with a bandanna tied across the lower portion of his face to shield him from that stinging dust, and with an ivory-butted six-gun lashed low along his right thigh. He was taller than his brother Frank had been and he looked to be possibly five years older, although now, with a day's growth of red-glinting whiskers over his face, he seemed much older than he actually was.

His eyes showed weariness down to their bluest depths and his shoulders also showed it, lying slackly beneath the jumper with its turned-up collar. He had strong cheek bones and long lips that came definitely together.

There was, too, deliberateness about Parker Travis; it plainly said that he took his time about all things. He was doing that now as he watched ahead for breaks in the swirling dust, was riding along as though he wished to forget nothing he saw, as though he thought it likely those yonder buildings, that old buffalo wallow there on his left, that quick lift of forested headland back beyond the ranch buildings, might offer him shelter or protection one day.

He measured distances, too, as he passed along. He noted brands, the quality of animals, their condition—shiny-coated or rough-coated. Very little got past him; he was observant and he had an excellent memory. It was these things which, several miles on, beyond that set of prosperous-looking ranch buildings, brought him up short, staring into a fenced pasture on his right where a blood bay horse stood head down and tail flattened, facing away from the wind.

For a little while the wind died in its gusty way, clearing the air between rider and blood bay horse. During this unpredictable interlude Parker Travis got down, walked over to the pasture fence, and stood there, fifty feet from the blood bay, gazing at him.

Behind Parker his seal-brown gelding keened the roiled air for a scent that was familiar to him, and nickered. The blood bay threw up its head, stared at man and horse, then moved tentatively toward both.

Parker's eyes shone with gradual warmth. He stepped aside so that his gelding could move up, could rub nozzles with the horse across the fence, and he said: "Well, boys, it's been a long trail, a hot and a hard one . . . but you two didn't forget, did you? I guess brothers always remember." He stepped up quietly, put forth a hand, and gently scratched the blood bay's neck. "You've looked better," he said. "Red, I'd give a lot of money if for just ten minutes you could talk." He dropped his hand and stepped back to run an assessing look over the blood bay. "Looks like you're recovering from a limp, Red. Maybe you fell. Maybe you stepped in a hole. And maybe a bullet nicked you." He looked out over the plain, slowly swinging his gaze so that it blocked in big chunks of range as a stockman does in a strange land, tracing out fence lines to determine limits and owner-ships.

"It's the big ranch we just passed that claims you now, isn't it?" he idly said to the blood bay horse, then he pulled his geld-ing away from the fence, stepped up, and reined away. The blood bay softly nickered at them from beyond the fence. Parker looked back.

"Rest easy, Red. We've found you now an' we'll be back. Don't you fret any about that . . . we'll be back."

For a little while, for as long as the pasture fence ran unobstructed, the blood bay gelding walked along it, keeping pace with the horse and rider upon the other far side of the fence. Where it cornered and an intersecting row of posts hung with wire ran northward, the blood bay had to stop. He lifted his head, gravely watched the rider move away. He softly nick-ered again.

Southward, on his left, Parker eventually made out the hot reflection of sunlight off windowpanes, off tin roofs, off scarcely turning windmills. This, he knew, would be his destination, the village of Laramie. He angled a little toward it, not certain yet in his mind what he meant to do.

Thus far he had spoken his name to no one. He had avoided the road, the ranches, even the occasional other riders he'd seen. Perhaps these precautions were pointless, but he reasoned that, when a man is riding toward probable trouble in a new land, prudence is his best recourse.

All Parker knew of his brother's passing was what he'd read in a Colorado newspaper brought south upon an Overland stagecoach. The only detail given in that account that had never left his thoughts since he'd seen that paper was the statement that Frank was an outlaw, that he'd robbed an express office at Laramie of $12,000—and that he had been afterward run down and shot to death by a posse. The same article said that a sheriff named Kenneth Wheaton had also died in that battle.

A man doesn't raise a brother as Parker Travis had raised Frank without knowing him. Frank had always been a cheerful, pleasant person, generous to a fault, loyal and faultlessly honest. If there had ever been anything about Frank that hadn't rung true, Parker would have known it. There never had been, so now he was approaching Laramie to learn more concerning his brother's killing.

But Parker Travis was not a fierce or savage man. He was not a killer nor was he riding any vengeance trail. He wanted to know the facts, and, if afterward someone was definitely at fault, he would do what he had to do. But, being close to thirty years old, Parker Travis rushed into nothing. That was why he now employed the caution that put him upon the outskirts of Laramie on this gusty, raw-hot day, riding his seal-brown thoroughbred horse—the brother to the blood bay back at Lincoln Ranch.

He removed his jumper, tied it aft of the cantle atop his bedroll, eased down into town from the north where the stage road also entered, went along to the livery barn, and dismounted to stand, stamping dust off until a hostler came to take his horse.

The hostler, a man with an eye for horseflesh, stood back a moment gazing upon the seal-brown. "We don't get many animals like him in here," he said to Parker, approving of the thoroughbred's appearance beneath layered dust. "You come a long way, mister, yet he's fresh as when he started out." The hostler reached for Travis's reins. "It sort of makes my day when a feller brings in a horse he's favored on the trail."

"Rub down," said Parker, turning away from the horse with saddlebags and bedroll over his shoulder, "grain, green hay, and clean water. All right?"

"Yes, sir." The liveryman beamed. "Tie stall or box stall?"

Parker looked at his horse. "Box stall," he said.

"Confidentially I'd have put him in one anyway." The hostler smiled. "The boss ain't in town today an' this kind o' quality deserves the best whether his owner can pay for it or not."

Parker's solemn regard softened toward this man who also had a soft spot for horseflesh. He wordlessly dug out two silver dollars and passed them over. "One for you," he said. "One on the bill until I settle up." He hitched at the load upon his shoulder, turned, and walked out into the brassy daylight. Around him Laramie was sweeping dust away from doorways and profanely wiping it from eyes.

He entered the Antlers Hotel, wrote the name "Bill Jones" in the register, paid for a room and a bath, and hiked upstairs, located his allotted quarters by a number upon the door, and entered. Across the roadway and downward from Parker's room, easily visible through the window, was the express office. He cast a glance over there and saw two men standing in shade, speaking together. One was a gray-haired burly man expensively dressed and very dark from exposure. His companion was tall and tough-looking with a long jaw and a thoughtful look to him. This second man held Parker Travis's attention particularly because of the little nickel badge upon his shirt front.

Later, Parker had his bath, re-dressed himself in fresh clothing, and went out on to the plank walk to take the measure of Laramie. By then it was blisteringly hot and breathless out. By then, too, the wind was entirely gone.

He looked for the gray-headed man and the sheriff again, failed to see either, and strolled once down and once back, considering the town. Laramie was a thriving village and it was also a talkative one. When he entered the Great Northern Saloon where an even dozen men were indifferently loafing, crossed to the bar and asked for cold ale, Johnny Fleharty served it himself. He also smiled disarmingly and mentioned the chief topic of local conversation—the weather.

"Hot again today," he said cheerfully, as a man might speak who not only does not have to go out into the heat himself, but also as a man who benefits from the thirsts of those who do have to be out in it. "An' that damned wind didn't help any, did it?"

Parker shook his head. He took up the glass, studied Johnny over the rim, and drained it empty, set it down, and put a big palm over it, indicating he did not wish for a refill. "Not usual for a wind like that to blow this time of year," he said, watching Johnny.

"Sure isn't." Johnny drew another ale, shot the glass southward along the bar to a hulking, drowsy man who was leaning there with his hat back, with oily hair low across his brow, and a bristly chin cupped in one hand while he solemnly considered the reclining nude behind Fleharty's bar. The cowboy caught the mug and held it still.

"Usually a thunderstorm comes with those summer winds," Johnny said, appraising Parker Travis with his bright glance. "This time . . . just more heat."

"A man'd have to have a good reason for riding in weather like this," commented Parker. "Like runnin' from the law or trying to find water."

Fleharty nodded. Parker saw a conversational germ take root in Johnny's mind. "Water's no problem on the Laramie Plains. We got plenty of water. But runnin' from the law, now that's something else again. I expect you saw in the papers where our express office was robbed a few weeks back."

Parker started to murmur something, but Johnny, who was quite a talker, pushed right on over this little fading sound.

"I was out with that posse, mister. It was at least a hundred and fifty in the shade." Johnny grinned. "An' no shade."

"Hundred and twenty," mumbled the drowsy big man down the bar, correcting Fleharty.

"All right, Ace, a hundred and twenty." Fleharty looked at Parker Travis. "I always say hot is hot. It can be a hundred and twenty or it can be a hundred and fifty . . . a feller suffers just as much from one as the other."

The loafing big man down the bar muttered again. "An' you weren't with the posse, either. You come later with your buckboard."

This time Johnny had to work at keeping up his smile. He considered Ace McElhaney for a silent moment, then lifted his shoulders, dropped them, and swung away. "What I was getting at, mister," he said to Parker. "That feller who robbed the express office run from the law, and, like you said, that's the only kind of a man who'd ride in weather like this."

"Seems to me," Parker drawled, as though making an effort to recall something half forgotten, "you boys got that man."

Johnny vigorously bobbed his head at this. "Yes, sir. But don't you know that outlaw was mounted on a thoroughbred horse and he led the posse for darn' near . . . . How long was it, Ace, before you an' Charley caught up with him?"

From down the bar that gruff voice came back slurred. " 'Bout four hours, I'd say."

Johnny looked triumphant. "Four hours. How do you like that for ridin' hard under this damned sun?"

Parker removed his palm from the empty glass and considered the wet ring in his hand. "Put up quite a fight, I heard," he mumbled without looking at Johnny.

"Like a lion," agreed Fleharty. "His horse fell in a 'dog hole an' hurt his leg or maybe the feller'd have got away."

"Like hell he would have," growled McElhaney.

Johnny bridled at this. "Anyway, this Travis feller . . . that was his name . . . yanked off his saddle and forted up behind it." Johnny considered the empty glass. "Care for a refill?"

Parker nodded. "And a refill for the big feller down the bar, too," he said.

Johnny got the beer, placed the glasses in front of McElhaney and Parker Travis, swiped once at the bar automatically with a rag, then said: "He killed Ken Wheaton, our sheriff. Plugged him comin' in neat as a. . . ."

"He was on the ground, not comin' in," contradicted McElhaney again. He drew wearily up off the bar, half turned, and leaned sideways again. "Damn it, Johnny, after all you saw and all you heard, you still can't get the straight of it. Ken was pressin' Travis from the north. He'd jump up, run in, drop down to an' Injun-crawl. That's what he was doin' when Travis got up on to one knee, caught Ken plumb in his sights, an' let him have it."

Parker turned from a long look at his untouched glass to put a very dry, very steady gaze upon McElhaney. What he saw made no very good impression. Ace had been drinking beer and ale all day, from the loose, oily appearance of his face. His rider's butternut shirt was salt-stiff and great crescents of sweat darkened each armpit and for halfway down each side. He hadn't shaved in several days, either, as he returned Parker's regard.

"You talk like a man who was there," Parker said.

"I was there. Only three of us was within sight o' Travis when that big blood bay horse o' his stepped in the 'dog hole and went down. Ken Wheaton, Charley Swindin, and me."

"Tell him how it was," urged Johnny.

"Not a lot to tell," mumbled McElhaney. "Travis forted up behind his saddle. He had a Winchester. Ken went north, Charley went around behind him, an' I come in from the south."

"You killed him?"

McElhaney looked exasperated. "Everyone asks that. There were three of us firin' at him . . . until Ken got knocked over. After that there was me an' Charley. But Travis started to fall right after he shot the sheriff. Maybe Charley got him, maybe I did, an' it's not plumb impossible that Wheaton's last slug struck him before he downed Wheaton." Ace shook his head in a lowered way, looking annoyed. "How the hell do you know in a battle like that who shoots who, I'd like to know, an' I'll tell you somethin' else, too. I'm getting sick an' tired of talkin' about it."

# V

The day after Parker Travis's arrival in Laramie he rode westerly out upon the plains. He was gone all day, and, when he returned, he had a handful of corroding brass cartridge casings, a piece of cloth from someone's shirt, and an indelible memory of the place where his brother had died fighting.

He took the things he'd found out there to his room, put them carefully upon a table, dragged a wired-together old chair to the front window, and sat there until night's cooling breezes came to mingle with the scorched scents of a dead day that lingered on throughout the night.

Later, he cleaned up and went down to the hotel's dining room, ordered supper, and killed the wait by drinking all the water he could pack under his dehydrated hide. He let all his muscles turn loose; it was a luxuriant feeling after suffering under the scalding sun all day. When his meal came, he realized that he had not been entirely aware of just how hungry he was until he actually smelled the food. Afterward, he evinced no hurry to depart. This was the first decent dining room table he'd pushed his boots under since leaving Arizona weeks earlier. The people coming and going, eating and speaking back and forth, fresh-scrubbed people in clean clothing, lifted his spirits a little. So did the meal. He sat on thoroughly enjoying this foreign atmosphere, was still sitting there, smoking one of those black Mexican cigars with his eyes drawn out narrowly with little shrewd lines around them, when a thick-shouldered, gray-headed man and a lithe tall woman passed up to the dining room entrance, and paused there.

He recognized the man at once as the same person who had been speaking to Laramie's sheriff in front of the express office the day before. But the rusty-haired, smoky-eyed woman he had never seen before; the high fullness of her upper body sang across that room to him, enlivening his every male instinct. Her wide mouth with its heavy-centered lower lip lay calmly closed, and her dead-level gaze, running over the room, which reminded him of smoke on a winter day, dropped once to his face, passed on, then came slowly back again. Her gaze though was cool, her manner indifferent. She had caught his unwavering regard; now she was returning it.

The older man spoke at her side indicating a table. The spell was broken, the two of them passed along into the room, and Parker removed his Mexican cigar to consider thoughtfully its inch-long dead ash.

The urges of a lone man always moved like the needle of a

compass to consideration of a beautiful woman, and afterward, perhaps a lifetime later, if her initial impression was strong enough, he could recall her in each handsome detail exactly as he'd seen her that one time.

Parker, with his back to that couple, did that now, considered Amy Morgan as he'd seen her beside Lew Morgan that little moment in the dining room doorway. Later, when he arose and nearly passed out of the room, he turned suddenly and saw her glance following him. Over all those heads and unnoticed, they looked straight at one another. Amy didn't look away; she caught his gaze and held it, seemingly appraising him, her face composed, her gaze cool, and after a time her eyes showed a little flare of surprise at his boldness, a little lift of interest.

He turned and walked on out of the room, a big compact man who moved with a rolling gait and a determined, deliberate onward thrust.

Amy touched Lew's arm. "That man leaving the room . . . who is he?"

Lew looked up and around, saw only the sweep of wide shoulders, and shook his head. "I don't know, I'm sure. Just a traveler possibly. This time of year Laramie gets its share of stock buyers and what-not."

Lew stopped speaking as Hub Wheaton came up, nodded, and smiled downward. "Glad to see you in town, Miss Amy," he said. "You're looking pretty as a May flower."

Amy smiled and Lew reached far over to draw forth an empty chair. "Sit down," he said. "Had your supper?"

Hubbell said he had but he sat, and, when a waiter came around, he asked for a cup of coffee. While he waited, he looked at Lew and said: "You're quite a fancier of horseflesh. If you have a minute after supper, I'd like you to walk over to the livery barn and look at an animal with me."

"Sure," said Morgan casually. "You looking for another saddle animal, Hub?"

"No. No, the one I've got is good enough for me. At least for now. Just want your opinion about something is all."

Lew, sensing nothing here, went ahead with his meal, but Amy was slower to abandon her study of the sheriff's melancholy face.

They talked of casual things until the meal was over. They left the dining room as a trio, went out to where Lew had his top-buggy, and there they drove northward and across to the livery barn.

"I'll only keep him a minute," said Hubbell Wheaton to Amy, as he climbed out and turned to look back. He seemed to be balancing something in his mind. In the end he didn't say it; he only nodded and walked around the rig where Morgan was waiting. Together they passed out of sight between two smoking carriage lanterns into the barn's gloomy interior.

Amy watched riders pass through alternate splashes of light and dark around her on the roadway. She heard the tinkling laugh of a saloon woman come out of the Great Northern, and she saw the stranger leaning idly against an overhang upright, smoking another black cigar and looking out into the westerly velvet night as though unconscious of everything around him, as though entirely lost to everything except his thoughts. He did not stir or drop his gaze, even when two rowdy cowboys swung past behind him. Her interest quickened again, seeing him like that. Then he did an entirely unexpected thing. He stepped down off the plank walk and strolled purposefully toward the Lincoln Ranch buggy. At the last moment, though, when Amy was positive he had seen her, had recognized her, and was going to speak, he swung out and around, passed behind the rig, and appeared upon the far side, walking past her uncle and Hubbell Wheaton where they were emerging from the barn. After that

he was lost to her. The next moment her uncle mumbled—
"Good night."—to Hubbell Wheaton, grunted up into the rig,
freed the lines, kicked off the foot brake, and clucked at the
horse between the shafts.

Lew drove well beyond Laramie out on to the prairie before
either of them spoke. There was the beginning of a full moon
above. Star shine lay silver-soft over everything and mantled the
distant dark-cut mountains with an eerie paleness.

"There's a thoroughbred horse in town," Lew said abruptly,
without any preamble at all. He swung his head. "That doesn't
mean anything to you, though, does it?"

Amy shook her head and leaned back. There was something
to a night such as this one that stirred her, made her restless
and dissatisfied.

"The blood bay is a thoroughbred, Amy."

Gradual understanding came now. She rolled her head upon
the seat back to look, hard, at her uncle. It was not what he had
said, but what he had not said that encouraged her to say: "And
the owner of this other thoroughbred . . . ?"

"Hub's going to find out. He just happened by tonight. The
hostler called him over, invited Hub to look at one of the finest
specimens of horseflesh the hostler had ever seen. It was this
thoroughbred."

"Hub thought of the blood bay?"

"Not right off. He said it struck him an hour later when
Johnny Fleharty was telling him how a stranger in town asked
Ace McElhaney if he had killed that Travis feller."

Amy said no more. She rolled her head in the opposite direction and solemnly looked up where stars like flung-back tears
shone with diamond brightness.

Lew was also quiet. When they arrived back at Lincoln
Ranch, he saw her to the main house door, then muttered
something about caring for the horse, and was gone two hours,

long enough to feed and bed down twenty horses.

Amy did not remain indoors. It was too still and stiflingly hot. She went out into the rose garden behind the house, sat down there in a little arbor, and heard a timber wolf cry in the far distance, this sound coming faintly in its sad, sad way down the hushed long miles.

The warnings were going out, she thought. Hubbell Wheaton had been first, then her uncle, and now, she was certain, Lew had gone to the bunkhouse, taken Charley Swindin outside, and had told him, too.

She stood up. She paced across the yard and back again. Her restlessness was stronger than ever. Finally she turned rigid in soft shadows, looking at the rear of the house. Inside, someone was moving about. A light came on in her uncle's bedroom. He had, she knew, come back from caring for the horse, which meant that once more a chain reaction was in motion. *They never learn,* she told herself with bitterness. *They had only last month buried their sheriff and a man whose luck had run out upon the Laramie Plains, and now they were firing one another up to repeat the same blind blunder all over again. They never learn.*

She made a slow swing of the garden and beyond it out into the yonder ranch yard. She had no purpose in doing this except the driving restlessness that possessed her.

She had no purpose at any rate until she stopped out there, looking beyond the orange-lighted bunkhouse where Swindin and her uncle's other riders lived, straight at the immense wooden barn where it stood, moon-shadowed in soft gloom.

The idea came in a rush. Her uncle was retiring. The men at the bunkhouse were also bedding down. If any of them thought of her at all, they would think she had also gone to her room. No one would stop her; no one would miss her.

She was halted, woman-like, for a detaining second while she considered how she was dressed, for supper in town at the hotel dining room, not for racing down the night on her horse. But Amy Morgan was direct in thought and action. She dismissed this notion and struck out deliberately for the barn.

It required very little time to saddle up, to rig out her horse and mount it, to go quietly out of the barn's rear opening on to the plain beyond, make a wide circuit, and eventually come upon the stage road, then to ease her horse over into a long lope and feel the whip of good night air against her burning face.

The ride into Laramie never seemed long in a buggy. Even at other times when she'd gone in on horseback, it had never appeared to take as long as it did this night. When it appeared that she'd never arrive, the few late-hour lights sprang up out of the onward night, burning yellow in the otherwise natural light. She slowed at Laramie's north end, looked right and left, then paced along to the livery barn where her uncle and Hub Wheaton had looked at the thoroughbred horse. There, she turned in on her lathered mount, came under the astonished stare of the night hawk, and asked at once who owned the thoroughbred horse.

The nighthawk was an elderly, paunchy man known only as Toby. His face very clearly said that he was now nonplussed at Amy Morgan's being out this late unescorted, in a fine gown, and looking as though she'd been racing in the moonlight.

"The thoroughbred . . . ?" he said blankly, not at once drawing his scattered thoughts together. "Oh . . . you mean the brown thoroughbred."

Amy nodded. She had no idea of the animal's color, had in fact never seen him, but there couldn't be two thoroughbreds in the livery barn, so she said: "Yes, the brown thoroughbred."

"Well, Miss Amy, as far as I know it's some feller stayin' over at the hotel. Feller named Jones . . . or was it Smith? No, it was Jones."

Amy sprang down, tossed her reins to the night hawk, and

ran lightly across the darkened roadway. Toby stood there, gaping after her until she disappeared between the globe lights on either side of the hotel's entrance. Then he blinked at her horse, slowly wagged his head back and forth in a scandalized fashion, and led the animal in out of sight. It was quite late. There was little chance of anyone's seeing the horse much less recognizing it as Amy's in the night gloom, but a man of Toby's age and ironbound proprieties preferred not to take any risks at all.

He was sitting on a horseshoe keg, looking as solemn as an owl, when Amy came hurriedly back, thanked him, sprang up, and wheeled out of the barn in a long lope.

# VI

Parker Travis was by habit and inclination an early riser. Even in a land where all men arose at sunup or shortly after, he was an early riser. He did not know it, but this long-standing habit kept him from a grilling by Hub Wheaton, for as soon as he appeared in the lobby, the night clerk came over and handed him an unaddressed envelope.

"Left for you last night . . . or early this mornin' . . . whichever you prefer."

Parker stood, gazing at the envelope. The clerk stood there, too. Parker dredged up a coin, dropped it into the clerk's hand, and walked on out into the predawn coolness of the empty, hushed roadway. He knew no one in Laramie.

It occurred to him, after his surprise abated, that the letter was not intended for him at all, that it was meant for someone else and had been mistakenly handed to him.

He gazed up the road and down the road. There was no one abroad. Laramie was quiet as a tomb. He went along to a bench, dropped down, broke open the envelope, and drew forth, not a note at all, but a hastily drawn map. The only writing on it was at a place that had been encircled. There it said simply: **I'll be waiting here at ten o'clock.**

There was no signature, either. Parker's brows ran together in a perplexed frown. He studied the map, made sense from it, then closely examined both map and envelope for some hint of the sender. There was none.

He sat a while, putting pieces of this puzzle together in his mind's eye, and came to a sound conclusion. He remembered his trail into Laramie vividly enough; he could check off each blaze on that trail against landmarks on the map. They led him eastward back beyond that big ranch where Frank's blood bay was. After that, he did not know the land at all, but he recalled the peaks and forms well enough to be confident of locating the spot indicated by those written words. It was somewhere deep in the forested foothills where the Laramie Plains were pinched out by mountain flanks.

He stood up. The town was still except for a rooster crowing in the middle distance. The sun was not yet up, would not be up for another hour. He paced thoughtfully over the roadway onward toward the livery barn.

No, he told himself, this was no mistake. There was a connection of some kind between the blood bay's new home and the appointed meeting. The longer Parker considered this, the more convinced he became. Obviously the meeting place was within the confines of that big ranch where his brother's horse now was. Someone out there, someone with a reason, wanted to see him.

He halted where the liveryman stumped forward to yawn and nod—then turn stiff all over. Parker, an observant man, noticed this quick change. He waited, giving the night hawk time to speak. When no words came, he wrinkled his eyes at the night hawk and said: "What's your name?"

"Toby."

"I'll remember that," Parker said, strode on past, and went along to rig out his mount, step over leather, and strike out of Laramie in a northward direction. He paused once to look back. Toby was in the doorway. He sucked back instantly, whipping out of sight. Parker swung back forward and continued on out of town. He didn't smile but he felt a little exultant. Someone had guessed who he was. From that it wouldn't be hard to guess why he was here. He reined east upon the stage road, thinking that in a small, garrulous place like Laramie it wouldn't be long before everyone connected with his brother's killing would be remembering or fabricating personal excuses and defenses. The word would spread like wildfire.

He speculated a little, as he rode through the faultless gray softness of predawn, on the identity of the person who had discovered his identity. He also wondered how this had come about. Well, a man's footsteps on earth may not be enduring, but as long as he's around to leave them, other men will watch him, think about him, rummage for his secrets and his motives. He had to let it lie like that because, so far, he had met only one person to whom his presence had been electrifying: Toby, the hostler back in town. Of course, there were others, but thus far he'd encountered none of them.

Where Lincoln Ranch's boundary lay, marked by a stone cairn, Parker considered the richness of that good land. Later, when buildings were in faint sight, he knew that before this day was past he would meet another one who knew his identity, someone connected with that large cow outfit.

He came even with the pasture fence where the blood bay had been, saw that he was no longer in that enclosure, and to break the monotony of this ride lifted his gelding into an easy lope.

When he slowed his mount a mile beyond Lincoln Ranch's hushed buildings, the land began to lift a little, to break into gentle rolls and adobe gulches. Still farther he encountered individual pine trees standing as sentinels to the onward hills. A very faint pink streak stained the eastern horizon, widening, broadening, altering its color chameleon-like until the palest blue imaginable began to tint the eastward heaven.

The hills came on to meet him, bulky, coarse, and crumpled, their deeper cañons still holding that night smokiness that was elsewhere beginning to give way before the paling eastern sky. Where he came upon a shallow creek with glass-clear water and visible gray pebbles on its bottom, he paused to offer his animal water. The horse drank, rinsed his mouth, and stood a moment, head still down, looking ahead where the first forest tier began.

He had left the stage road a mile back, had swung northeast while the road meandered slightly southeast. But even so, at this shallow ford where he now sat, there were signs that this crossing was much used. He found tracks that were no older than the day before. Under these tracks were older ones. He was interested in determining how many riders had passed up into the hills recently. Yesterday there had been only that one rider. Other times there had obviously been several at a time.

Out upon the Laramie Plains the sun jumped up, a faint-lighted world turned abruptly bright, hard yellow, and another sizzling day had commenced. In the forest that light came cathedral-like, long, broad beams of it spilling in arrow-straight lines where it could get through stiff-topped pines, and lie golden upon the carpeted floor. It found Parker Travis now and then, where he passed across openings, caught his shadow, and made it run on ahead.

He plodded along through the peacefulness of this cool, soft-shadowed place with the blue jay always 100 yards ahead making his warning cry. The trail passed through a damp clearing where forest ferns grew stirrup high. Here, because these ferns were jungle-like plants that covered tracks within days, he had to dismount and feel his way along ahead of his horse.

The trail upon the fern bed's far side emerged and went, faintly discernible, into the forest again. It rose sharply over a hogback, plunged into a narrow little gloomy cañon, swung suddenly due north, and ran along a shale ridge for 100 yards, then angled downward again into a secret dell where a creek ran brawlingly southward. Here, it seemed to end.

Parker tied his horse where trees were thick and darkness still lay. He unshipped his carbine, paced up to the very edge of that little glen, and halted to stand a long time, just looking. Neither making a sound nor moving at all, just looking.

Someone visited this place often, and yet, although he had no difficulty tracing out the pathways this person had made, he found no indication of fresh human sign, or that which he particularly sought—an established place of concealment.

He stepped out into the glen. He stepped along to the creek, halted, stared downward, put aside his Winchester, and dropped to one knee. The boot track there was no more than twenty-four hours old, which did not surprise him, but it was small, narrow, delicate—which did surprise him. He stood upright, reached for his carbine, and looked a moment at the hurrying little white-water creek. This secret place was not the refuge of a man at all. This belonged to a woman! No man had feet that small or that made so light an imprint upon creekbank soil.

He returned to his horse, brought it down into the glen where emerald grass was plentiful, loosened the *cincha*, dropped the reins, and left the animal to hike back to that shale rock ledge. There, he hunted a cool vantage point, sat upon a punky deadfall pine, and made a long, careful study of the land formation around him. Far off he could distinguish where the Laramie Plains ran westward from the mountains.

He had a feeling of safety in here. Partly this came from solid knowledge. On the way in he'd watched the trail, no one had preceded him, no one had branched off to circle around and perhaps lay an ambush. But it was the great depth of silence, of unchanging serenity that went down deeply into him, giving full reassurance as he sat there, Winchester across his knees, hat back and muscles loose, studying this land, getting the hang of it out of habit, remembering distances, landmarks, lifts and rises.

It was so totally quiet that when the blue jay broke out down-country, angrily denouncing some trespasser, Parker's heart momentarily thudded. He sat like stone listening to the bird, by its course tracing out the route of whatever was entering this quiet world.

He did not readily accept the notion that whoever had summoned him to this meeting was coming, for the simple reason that it was too early in the day yet. Then he heard a horse clear its nostrils, and after that he heard a shod hoof strike stone. He rose up, glided onward to an overlooking rib of land, faded out in shadows there, and waited. Below him the trail passed across that unobstructed fern patch.

The camp robber came winging; it flashed iridescent blue, settled upon a low limb and scratchily kept up its loud scolding. Horse and rider appeared crossing the fern patch. Parker, lightly dappled, half shadowed, half not, unmoving, waited until he had a good sighting. He let off a soft sigh. It was a girl and he recognized her, the girl who had been in the hotel dining room.

He remained where he was. She passed beyond sight into a little shallow gully, then he heard her horse working upward again, coming straight along the path that lay only 100 feet off on his right. He did not move. Suddenly the beast heaved up over its last obstacle, moving along head down, reins swinging, obviously using a trail with which it was entirely familiar. The girl was riding easily in her saddle; she was wearing a rusty-colored split skirt and a lighter tan shade of blouse. Her deep-colored hair was caught at the back of her head and held in place by a little green ribbon. She swung her head, looked straight at Parker, and passed by without any break in expression at all. She had not seen him.

# VII

Parker let Amy get well along before he stepped forth to pace after her to the dell's outer limits. There, he stood back watching her, awaiting the reaction certain to come when she spied his horse grazing in the glen.

She received advance warning, though, for when her mount caught horse scent and flung up its head, Amy understood at once, halted, sat a second, then got down.

That was when Parker took two big steps and came up behind her. He had the map in his right hand, the Winchester in his left. He said quietly: "You're a good topographer, ma'am. I had no trouble at all."

She whipped around, startled by his close appearance. Her gray eyes darkened to almost black. He stood there, seeing her up close for the first time. He could not find a flaw.

Then she recovered, dropped her gaze to the map, considered it very briefly, turned away from him, and moved ahead with her horse into the quiet glen. He paced along behind her, also saying nothing. They stopped where she saw his horse, stood a while gazing steadily at it, then turned to care for her own. He did not intrude but moved over where a crumbling log lay, leaned his Winchester there, sat down, and kept watching her, kept waiting.

She turned, gazed across at him, and said with a slight edge to her voice: "Are you always early, Mister Travis?"

He tossed his hat aside. Some of that outside heat was beginning to creep up into this place. "Didn't you know," he said dryly to her, ignoring her question, "that my name on the hotel register is Jones?"

She walked over to him, stood gazing down without any trace of self-consciousness. "It's Travis, isn't it?"

Parker nodded. "Parker Travis, ma'am. How did you know?"

"The horse, Mister Travis. Two thoroughbred horses showing up in Laramie within a month or six weeks of each other is unusual."

"You know horses that well, ma'am?"

"No. My uncle does, though. He and Sheriff Wheaton and a liveryman in town."

"I see. They pieced it together."

"Yes."

"Well, it's not illegal to ride a thoroughbred horse on the Laramie Plains, is it?"

She didn't answer that, instead, she moved to one side and sat down upon the same old log. "You haven't asked me my name or why I sent you that map, Mister Travis."

He twisted a little to look at her. He thought he'd never before encountered a woman like this one. She had the ability to draw him; she also had everything that aroused in men every male instinct. But there was more and he could not right then define it.

He said: "You'll tell me in good time, when you explain why you sent for me, why you made the meeting this private."

She looked around at him from beneath black lashes, her expression appraising, her eyes the slightest bit sardonic. "It's all right to be fatalistic," she said. "But not when it can get you killed."

"You're misreading me, ma'am. It's not fatalism. It's patience. If it'd been fatalism, I wouldn't have arrived here early to scout the country. I'd have taken my chances and ridden in here with no second thoughts."

She continued to study him. After a little silent interval she said: "Perhaps I misjudged you, Mister Travis. But that's not important right now." She paused, looking at him, giving him a chance to speak. He kept still, kept quiet, looking at her.

She drew in a breath. "Mister Travis . . . will you honestly answer a question for me . . . a personal question?"

"I'll try, ma'am."

"Where did Frank Travis get nine thousand dollars in gold?"

Without any hesitation Parker said: "He got it from the sale of land he and I jointly owned. Nine thousand dollars was his share." Parker drew forth his wallet, extracted a worn, folded paper, and offered it. "This will confirm it. This is a copy of the deed we granted the man who bought that land for cash."

Amy looked at the folded paper in his hand, then up again. She made no move to take the paper. "Am I allowed one more question?"

Parker nodded.

"Was your brother ever in trouble with the law?"

"No, ma'am. My folks died when Frank was pretty young. I raised him. He's never been in any serious trouble. A few bar-room fights, a little illegal horse racing on Sunday. That's all of it." Parker put the paper and his wallet away. He raised his eyes to Amy's face, and the two of them exchanged a long look before he said: "Now I'd like some answers. I know who two of the men are who were out there the day my brother was shot to death. Ace McElhaney and Charley Swindin. Tell me something about those two."

Amy looked at the hands in her lap. "Ace McElhaney is a cowboy. He works for the big outfits, but, when he gets a little money ahead, he hangs around town."

"And Swindin?"

"Well," said Amy, concentrating very hard upon her folded hands now. "He's foreman of the Lincoln Ranch."

"The Lincoln Ranch, ma'am?"

Amy explained where her uncle's outfit was.

Parker nodded, his interest fully up now. "I see, ma'am," he said. "I'm beginning to put some little pieces together."

"What pieces?"

"Yesterday I saw my brother's blood bay horse in a Lincoln Ranch pasture."

"Yes, he's there."

"Any you . . . you're connected with Lincoln Ranch some way?"

"I'm Lew Morgan's niece. Lew owns Lincoln Ranch."

"Uhn-huh," murmured Parker. "Now, Miss Morgan, you didn't call me up here because you want to give me back my brother's horse. I don't even believe you called me up here to warn me against Swindin."

Amy's gaze turned liquid-dark. "Why did I ask you to meet me here, Mister Travis?"

"Because someone down at Lincoln Ranch was involved in Frank's killing."

Amy nodded gravely. "Go on."

"You want to head off violence. Whoever he is at Lincoln Ranch, you don't want him killed."

"My uncle, Mister Travis," said Amy, and explained.

Parker listened. Near the end of Amy's recitation, he lit a Mexican cigar and quietly smoked. When she had finished speaking, he still silently smoked. Finally, looking at cigar ash, he spoke. Each word fell like steel upon glass. "They could've hailed my brother, ma'am. They could have given him a chance after his horse went down." He shot her a challenging look. She met it but not in the same temper. "They could've made him give up. You said that posse had thirty men in it. No single man, no matter how good he is with guns, would in his right mind try to fight thirty men."

"But only McElhaney and Swindin were up there, Mister Travis. The others didn't come along until later."

"My brother was afoot, ma'am. He couldn't have gone anywhere. All McElhaney and Swindin had to do was wait. That's all. Just sit there and wait until the others came up. Frank, no matter what he believed, would not have died for that nine thousand dollars."

"What do you mean . . . no matter what he believed?"

"Miss Morgan, I don't know your uncle or those other men, but I *did* know my brother. If he had believed they were posse men, he never would have tried to outrun them. Never."

Amy watched him. She was still now and totally silent, with her lips lying closed in gentle fullness. Her eyes were very dark and he could not read expression in them.

"Why are you here, Mister Travis, to kill them?"

She was round-shaped in his sight; the pull of her was urgent. He fought against it, forcing his mind to that other thing between them.

"If need be, Miss Morgan. If need be."

"You are the judge?"

"I am the judge."

She said in a small, soft tone. "What will it solve . . . your way?"

"Perhaps nothing, ma'am. Perhaps a lot. You have no brother, no children?"

She dropped her eyes to her lap briefly, then raised them. "I have never been married."

"Then you wouldn't know how it is with me, because you see, ma'am, Frank was both, and he was needlessly killed."

"Yes," she breathed, seeing him draw together, hardening against her, and wanting this least of all. "Yes, I understand how it is with you. I knew it when you didn't ask what became of the money. You weren't interested in that . . . only in your brother."

"You're on the other side," he said, making it almost a query. "I'm sorry about that."

"Why should you be?"

He was temporarily stopped cold by her directness, yet he could see that this was how she was. He hung fire over his answer, though, and replied belatedly and slowly: "It doesn't matter right now."

She waited for more to come. It never did, so she changed the subject. "The nine thousand dollars is at the express company. It's in the safe there."

He said indifferently: "That'll keep. What I want to know is what are the plans of your uncle and those other men . . . McElhaney and Swindin."

"I can't answer for any of them, not even my uncle. But I would like you to talk to him . . . first."

He did not miss that pause before her final word. "I'm not swollen with hate or anxious to kill, Miss Morgan," he stated. "I want justice, though, and I aim to see that it's served. If, as you've told me, Sheriff Wheaton is the brother of the former sheriff, then I may not get justice." He turned away from her. "But I hope that's not the case."

"These aren't bad men, Mister Travis. They made a terrible mistake. They aren't fully aware yet just how awful a mistake they made. But once they know who you are, they'll find out, because I know my uncle and I know Hubbell Wheaton . . . they'll come to you, they'll ask questions. That piece of paper you're carrying. . . ."

"Yes?"

"As I said, I know those men. They'll be sick when they know what they've actually done."

"Sicker," said Parker Travis, "much sicker than you know, ma'am, if they think talk will right the wrong."

Parker stood up. He turned and gazed down at Amy. She sat

there watching him. He looked at her eyes, saw something that had not been in their dark depths before, something glowing, something mysterious, and he did a bold thing. He said roughly: "Meeting like this, here today, belongs to other things than what we've spoken of. I wish it could have been different."

He went out to his horse, tugged up the rigging, mounted, and started on out of the glen. Amy stood up and watched him pass. When he was near the forest's fringe, she called to him.

"The only man who profits from killing is the man without a conscience."

He drew rein to look back at her briefly. He made no comment on what she'd said. "I'll see you again," he said, and rode on.

Beyond their meeting place the forest was turning warm, turning humid. He was conscious of this but not in a direct way; he was considering the things she'd said.

By the time he was back at the little shallow waterway beyond the turn-off to that secret place, he'd decided to see Lew Morgan and Hubbell Wheaton, but not their way if he could avoid it—not at any disadvantage—but *his* way, which would be separately and alone.

He halted in the last of the forest shade. Ahead lay the open country again, shimmering in layers of heat. Where the sun rode, near its meridian, was a blinding-yellow molten ball. Around it the heavens were seared white; farther out they were a brassy, faded color. He was not anxious to push on, but he did, and at once his horse had almost to lean into the gelatin waves that ran at him. It was well over 115 degrees out on the Laramie Plains.

He endured this withering heat by closing his mind to it, by allowing his horse to pick its own walking gait, and by riding easily in the saddle. In this manner he struck the stage road and kept to it until, only a little distance from Laramie, a coach rattled by, its driver up high on his seat burned brown, its horses sweated, trotting loosely, their eyes red-rimmed. He gave way, riding off the road. When the driver threw him a wave, Parker waved back.

Afterward, he followed, first the dust, then the hot, acrid smell of that dust, for another mile. As distance widened between them, heat waves made it appear that the coach was not upon the road at all, but was floating in air several feet above the road. He considered the phenomenon through narrowed eyes. Because everything onward was blurry in his sight, he thought he also saw another horseman far ahead who left the road to let the coach pass by. He considered this an illusion, though, a mirage, and paid it no attention.

The coach faded out. Only the smell of its passing remained. There was no further sign of that ghostly rider, and Parker's mind turned inward again, reviewing all the things Amy had said to him, reviewing Amy herself. He was riding like that, utterly loose, entirely apart from the seared world he was passing through, when the gunshot came, its unmistakable muzzle blast flat, lethargic in the thick heat.

# VIII

Ordinarily a man cannot move fast in that kind of heat, but Parker Travis was an Arizonan. Heat was a way of life to him. He was to a considerable extent inured to it.

He left his saddle, rolled once and stood up again, holding one split rein. His horse was surprised but not particularly startled. It stood peering around as Parker drew forth his Winchester.

The man who had fired that solitary shot was far out in the shimmering glow. He was riding southward now as though to go cautiously out and around Parker, but when he'd fired, he'd been in the westward roadway. That horseman had not been a mirage after all.

Parker turned his horse, keeping the beast in front of him so that the assassin could not at that distance determine whether Parker was shot down or not. He estimated the course of this unknown enemy, gauged the distance before the man would come into Winchester range, then sank down upon the ground to wait.

Through that long waiting period Parker speculated upon the assassin's identity. It seemed a fortuitous thing to him that his foeman had known where to find him, had appeared so soon after he'd left Amy Morgan. His thoughts turned upon the beautiful girl with no kindness at all. He was not angry, not in the way another man might have been, not with outrage and cold wrath. But he was getting that way as time passed. The uncomfortable hotness rose against him from out of the ground, and that extremely careful killer kept on riding slowly, cautiously, coming inward a little at a time.

Sweat ran into his eyes. He furtively flicked it away. He wanted that rider out there to believe he was dead or nearly so. He made no noticeable move while he was prone in the blasting heat, except to follow that man's progress down his gun barrel.

The unknown horseman stopped finally, sat his saddle, straining to see up where Parker lay. He was holding his bared saddle gun balanced upon one hip. The sun was well above him, making a minimal shadow. Parker estimated the distance. It was by his reckoning still a little too far. He swore to himself, suffering upon the oven-like ground.

The assassin made his decision, turned northward, and came on with no further delay. Parker watched him pass into range and did nothing. He let the man get within 1,000 yards of him, then he fired.

At first it was impossible to tell how badly he'd hit his enemy because his horse shied violently at the gunshot, nearly jerking free. Parker held tightly so that one split rein was jerked half around, and, when he looked back, the assassin's animal had also shied, had whipped completely out from under his rider, and was fleeing back toward Laramie now, head up and tail flying.

The stranger himself lay sprawled. His carbine was thirty feet away, glistening in the evil light. He was lying upon his back, staring straight up at the sun. From this and the fact that he did not move, Parker thought he must be dead. He was.

Parker got up to him. The man's face was serene beneath its dust-sweat coating, beneath its several days' growth of rusty whiskers. He had been downed by a slug directly through his heart. He had never known what had struck him.

Thirst came to torment Parker. He got the dead man behind his cantle, tied him there, mounted up, and resumed his onward journey. Under his leg in its boot rode his own gun; across his lap was the carbine of the dead man.

This was how he rode into Laramie. This is how people saw him who were sitting, idle and drained of energy, when he passed along to the sheriff's office, stiffly got down, tied his laden horse, and pushed on into Hubbell Wheaton's office to say thinly to the sad-faced man sitting at a desk there: "My name is Travis, which I'm sure you know, and, if you've the time, I'd like a few words with you." He did not mention the dead man outside. Wheaton motioned toward a chair and studied Travis with close interest.

"I was looking for you earlier this morning," said Hub, "but the livery barn hostler told me you rode out before sunup."

"You won't have to look any more, Sheriff. Neither will the others who're interested in my being here in your town."

"The others, Travis?"

Parker made a rueful little head wag. "You don't have to put on an act for my benefit, Sheriff. Charley Swindin was one of the men who murdered my brother. Lew Morgan was involved in it, also. So were you. I know each of you now, by name."

"We weren't the only ones, Travis. There were a lot of men in that posse. In fact, you didn't name one of the men who was actually up there when your brother died."

"I don't have to name that one," said Travis.

"No?"

"No. You see, he's paid his debt in full. He's outside, Sheriff, tied behind my saddle . . . dead."

Hub's gaze slowly widened. "Ace?" he said. "Ace McElhaney?"

Parker nodded. "I was coming back to town this morning. A Cheyenne coach passed me. Ahead of it was a horseman. At first I thought he might be a mirage in the heat." Parker paused slowly to wag his head. "He was no mirage. He took a long shot at me, missed, and I let him get up closer, then I killed him."

Hub got out of his chair, crossed to the door, flung it back, and stood in the opening, gazing out where Travis's thoroughbred stood patiently with his grisly burden. From behind him Parker said: "This is his carbine. You can see that it's been fired."

Hub turned, made no move to take the Winchester, and continued the study of Travis. Finally, still ignoring the carbine, he walked heavily back and dropped down into his chair again.

"Anyone see this fight?" he asked.

"No one."

Hub looked over where Parker had leaned the Winchester upon a wall. "I reckon, if a feller was dead set on makin' another man's killing look plumb legal when there were no witnesses, it wouldn't be hard for him to shoot the dead feller's gun once or twice after he'd killed him."

"It wouldn't be hard at all," agreed Parker, rising to stand there in the little breathless room. "It'll be a damned sight harder to prove that's how it was, though."

"Where are you going, Travis?"

"To toss McElhaney off my horse, put the animal up, then go drink a gallon of water. Why?"

"There's cold water in that bucket yonder. I'd like to talk to you. It shouldn't take long."

Parker paused in the doorway. A hot little wind was passing southward. Where he stood, it struck him, drying the sweat and making him feel cool. "Talk," he ordered.

"I don't know how McElhaney died, but I can guess, since you knew he was one of the men who shot your brother, that you weren't sorry to shoot him."

"You're partly right, Sheriff. I meant to look him up sooner or later . . . but not particularly to kill him. That would've been up to him. I just wanted him to tell me why he and Swindin . . . and all the rest of you for that matter . . . didn't give my brother a chance to surrender."

Hub Wheaton offered no explanation. He only said: "Travis, what about Charley Swindin? You know who he is, don't you?"

"I know. He is the other one."

"Well . . . ?"

"That'll be up to him, too, Sheriff." Parker started to pass on outside. He checked himself briefly and added: "That goes for every one of you who were involved in the murder."

"We didn't think it was murder."

Parker teetered there. Something Amy had said came back to him. He stepped back inside, drew forth a piece of paper, unfolded it, tossed it to Wheaton. "Read that," he said.

Wheaton bent to frown over the paper. He read it through once, took it in his hand, walked over to a little window, and re-read it. From there he gazed across somberly at Parker Travis. He pushed out his hand with the paper in it.

"Here," he said. "Take it. Go get your drink of water."

Parker left the office and did exactly what he'd said he meant to do. Under the staring eyes of a large number of townsmen who had drifted up to look at the limp body of Ace McElhaney, he untied the corpse, stepped aside to let it slide down into roadway dust, stepped over it without once looking down, and walked northward up the road, leading his horse toward the livery barn. Behind him, Sheriff Hub Wheaton and not less than twenty-five totally still and silent men watched him go.

Not always the most fragrant place in frontier towns, but certainly one of the coolest in summertime and also one of the most popular loafing places, the livery barn in Laramie was rarely vacant. When Parker walked in leading his thoroughbred, a number of idlers in the shade there, some whittling, some just sitting, put their unblinking gazes on him. These men had seen him ride into town; they had seen what he'd left lying in the naked sunlight down at Wheaton's jailhouse. They were very interested, but, also, they were very careful. Parker Travis had none of the look of a killer or a gunfighter, but mostly those loafers were not very young men, and therefore they had survived in a perilous land because they could make correct appraisals with their mouths closed. They did this now. They also saw at once how Toby, the hostler, flinched when he came up out of the dark runway to take Travis's horse.

Parker held out his reins. He looked thoughtfully at Toby, then he said: "The next time you send someone out after me, I'm going to come for you."

He turned, walked out of the barn, through that deep silence, across the dusty roadway, and on into the hotel. There, he removed his shirt in the privacy of the upstairs room he'd rented, beat dust out of it, washed his entire upper body, dried off by standing at the window looking solemnly down where Ace McElhaney was being carted off by several men, got into

129

the same shirt again, and went downstairs, on into the dining room, put his hat aside, and flagged a waiter. The man came with an alacrity he had not shown before when he'd served Travis.

He ordered a midday meal, a pitcher of water, then sat tanking up, waiting for the food. The first glass of water brought forth a veritable flood of perspiration. The second one winnowed away some of the rawness from his gullet, his mouth, and lips, and the third one soothed his spirit.

His table faced forward toward the outside door and the roadway beyond. He was idly looking out there when he saw a horseman go loping past northward. It was Sheriff Wheaton. He was riding too fast for this kind of weather. Parker inwardly smiled. It wouldn't take Wheaton long at that gait to reach Lincoln Ranch. He wished he had known Wheaton was going to do this. He'd have asked him to be sure and tell Morgan's niece her plot failed and that her assassin had himself been killed.

His lunch came. He began slowly to eat. From the edge of his vision he saw men pass quietly into the dining room and pass out again. Others, lacking this boldness, came only as far as the doorway to gaze at the man who had killed Ace McElhaney, then they also moved on. One man only seemed as though he wished to speak. In the end, though, this man, too, faded beyond Parker's sight. When the loitering waiter saw this man, he made a little gasp. Parker looked up at him, caught the waiter's eye, and crooked a finger.

"Who was he?" he asked.

"Who was who, sir?"

Parker leaned back, pushed his plate away, and put a sardonic look upward. "I'm waiting," he said very quietly. "Who was that man?"

"Uh . . . foreman for one of the ranches hereabouts, Mister Travis."

"I see. He wouldn't be foreman of Lincoln Ranch, would he, friend?"

The waiter's face turned white. "Please don't put me in this spot, Mister Travis."

"What spot?"

"Everyone in town knows who you are, sir. Word travels fast after a shootin'."

"I can see that it does. That was Charley Swindin, wasn't it?"

"Yes, sir," the waiter whispered, looking anguished. "Can I go now?"

Parker nodded. The waiter scuttled rapidly away, and those prying-eyed men disappeared from the doorways.

# IX

Toby, the aging hostler, was limply parked upon a horseshoe keg just inside the door where coolness lay. Upon both sides of the runway inside the barn were box stalls and tie stalls; from these gloomy slots came sounds of horses munching, stamping at flies, or rubbing.

Parker halted near Toby and considered him from a blank face. The hostler spoke up huskily at once, saying: "Hones' t'gawd, Mister Travis, I had no hand in Ace McElhaney goin' after you this morning. I can't make you believe that, but it's gospel truth."

"That's interesting," said Travis mildly. "You knew who I was when I came in here this morning."

"I wasn't the only one, Mister Travis. Hub Wheaton figured it out, too. So did Lew Morgan of Lincoln Ranch."

"Morgan wasn't in Laramie this morning before sunup, was he, Toby?"

The hostler heard skepticism in Travis's voice. "No, sir," he answered right back. "But Hub was, an' so was McElhaney. I don't know this, mind you, an' Sheriff Wheaton probably wouldn't like it if he heard me say it, but him and Lew Morgan saw your thoroughbred last night an' they talked about it."

"What of that?" asked Parker.

"Well, there's only one other thoroughbred in the country, and they suspicioned who you was from that. An' the first thing fellers do under circumstances like them is warn everybody else, ain't it?"

Parker thought on this, and after a moment he nodded. "It's possible, all right. Now tell me when you saw McElhaney the last time and who he was with?"

"I seen him last night over at Johnny Fleharty's saloon. Him and Johnny was talkin'."

"No one else, Toby?"

"On my honor, Mister Travis, just them two."

Without another word Parker strode out of the barn, across the hot roadway, and into Fleharty's Great Northern Saloon.

Fleharty was standing listlessly behind his bar, picking his teeth and gazing drowsily over at a poker game, the only source of interest in his place at this suppertime hour of the day. He saw Parker Travis come in and became at once alert and apprehensive. When Parker crossed to the bar and leaned there, looking over at him, Johnny said quickly, with a false smile: "Ale? I recollect you as an ale man."

"Who told McElhaney who I was?" Parker softly asked, cutting out the preliminaries.

The poker game had suddenly gone flat; those quiet-faced men over at the table were all looking straight up where Fleharty and Parker Travis stood. The saloon was quiet enough to hear each outside sound throughout its big barn-like room. Johnny Fleharty killed time drawing a glass of ale. He shot a look over at the poker players and turned red under their blank stares. He put the glass in front of Parker, made a mechanical sweep of his bar top with a rag, and lifted his eyes. Parker was watching him still; he was obviously awaiting his answer.

"Sheriff Wheaton knew who you were," he said at last, his voice scratchy. "I reckon a lot of folks knew, for that matter."

Parker pushed the ale aside. He shook his head at Fleharty. "Until last night they didn't. Who did McElhaney talk to last night?"

"How would I know, mister? Ace didn't spend all his. . . ."

"I want a straight answer from you," said Parker, drawing back a little from the bar as he interrupted. "Make it easy on yourself, Fleharty, or make it hard. It's up to you."

Johnny, who was a little man in many ways, screwed up his face in pure agony. If he answered, those listening poker players would hear him surrender. If he didn't answer, the killer of Ace McElhaney probably would do something about that. Johnny was at that crossroad many men face in a lifetime—he had either to sacrifice self-esteem and local respect, or perhaps his life. He wasn't sure this was so but he had to make his choice now, and the wrong decision could be dangerous. But Johnny was a small man so he made the safe decision by saying: "Sheriff Wheaton and Lew Morgan talked to Ace." He left off speaking, his breathing hurried, as though he was out of breath now.

Parker nodded. "One more question. Charley Swindin was in town a little while back. Did he come in here?"

"He usually does when he's in town," Johnny said, groping for some way to salvage some of that respect by seeking to evade another question. "Charley's been comin'. . . ."

"Was he in here this afternoon?"

There it was again, the blunt question from that unreadable, strong, and weather-darkened face. Johnny made another prolonging swipe with his bar rag. This time, though, like all men who have once given in, he had less difficulty answering.

"Yes, he was in here a little after noon."

"What did he say?"

"Well. He said you'd killed Ace. He said he knew who you were, because Lew Morgan told him last night at the ranch Frank Travis's brother was in town."

"What else?"

"Well, he said you weren't goin' to slip up from behind and get him like you got Ace."

Parker looked over at the poker players. There were six of them and they solemnly returned his look. "If any of you believe that's how McElhaney died, go look at him. Go see whether that bullet hit from behind or from in front."

None of the card players spoke. They sat on, though, appraising Parker. Johnny Fleharty looked at his fingertips. At this moment he despised himself, could not bring himself to look out at the man who had made that kind of a coward of him.

Parker wheeled about, left the saloon, and turned southward toward the hotel. He almost at once collided with Sheriff Wheaton. Hub stopped dead still. He was sweat-dust stained and red-necked.

Parker beat him to it. He said: "Have a nice ride to Lincoln Ranch, Sheriff?"

Hub shook his head, looking more mournful than ever. "No," he replied quietly, "it's hotter'n the hinges of hell on the plains today."

"Yeah," grunted Parker. "In more ways than one. What's on your mind?"

"I was looking for you."

"I can see that. What for . . . to arrest me?"

Hub Wheaton was not like Johnny Fleharty; he did not scare easily. "No. Not yet anyway. To tell you there's a man in the hall outside your hotel room waiting to talk to you."

Parker's mind selected a name and dropped it down. "Morgan?" he asked.

134

"Yes, Lew Morgan. He rode back with me. Are you going to see us?"

"I've already seen you, Sheriff. I'll see Morgan alone."

Parker started past. Hub Wheaton turned slowly to watch him progress southward. Once, he parted his lips to speak, then he closed them again and stood undecided while Travis swung in and passed beyond his sight at the hotel doorway.

Several men came out of the Great Northern Saloon. They saw Hub standing there and came to a rough stop. Johnny Fleharty also pushed through and saw Hub, but Johnny didn't hesitate at all; he rushed at the sheriff.

"Hub, that feller Travis was just in my place makin' me tell him about you warnin' Ace about him bein' in town an' that he was that other Travis's brother."

Wheaton swung back. Over Fleharty's shoulder he spied those rough range men standing together by the saloon's doorway. He read their faces and their stances correctly.

"What're you tryin' to do," he asked Johnny, "start a fight?"

Fleharty looked bewildered. "What are you talkin' about? I was in my own saloon mindin' my own business. . . ."

"I'm talking about those riders back there . . . those six men who just came out of your place. Who got them on the prod?"

"I didn't. It was Travis. They heard him pumpin' me about Charley Swindin an' you talkin' to Ace last night. You an' Lew Morgan. They. . . ."

"Lew Morgan wasn't in your place last night, Johnny."

Fleharty blinked. His agitation was considerable. "Wasn't he with you when you talked to Ace?"

"No, he wasn't."

"I thought . . . I guess there were too many fellers in there for me to be sure last night." Johnny's eyes widened. "I thought he was with you 'n' Ace. That's what I told Travis."

"No," growled Hub Wheaton. "You're not tryin' to stir

anything up. Hell, no, you're just tryin' to get Lew killed along with Swindin."

Fleharty said protestingly: "But, Hub. . . ."

Wheaton, however, was passing northward toward those six grim-faced cowboys up the sidewalk. He left Fleharty standing helplessly, with new sweat bursting out upon his face, feeling more degraded than ever.

When he was close to the motionless range riders, Wheaton said: "Forget it. There's enough trouble here without you fellers butting in."

One of those cowboys, a gaunt, battered man, hooked both thumbs in his shell belt, looked coolly at the sheriff, and growled: "You folks here in town afraid of that Travis feller?"

Hub's long face settled into tough lines. He said sarcastically: "Yeah, we're scairt to death of him. We're also scairt to death of men like you. We're so scairt I'm going to lock the lot of you up in my jailhouse unless you climb on your horses right damned now and hightail it out of town and back wherever you belong."

Another rider, broad, swarthy, raffish-appearing, looked around. He made an elaborate shrug with his shoulders and said gruffly to his friends: "To hell with it. Come on, let's get goin'. These here folks don't want no help." This man turned his back upon Hub Wheaton, stepped down into roadway dust, and trudged over where six saddled horses were drowsing. His friends went along after him, one at a time, until only the gaunt, battered man remained behind.

Hub took a little forward step, put his palm against this cowboy's chest, and gave a little push. The gaunt man's eyes flashed; he dropped both hands from his belt and teetered there, on the brink of action.

From his saddle, out in the yellow brilliance, that raffish-looking man called: "Forget it, Buck! Come on. Let the towns-folk handle it their own clumsy way."

"That," said Wheaton quietly to the angry-eyed man in front of him, "is damned good advice."

Afterward, when the six of them were riding off, Johnny Fleharty came up tentatively, not certain whether to speak or step on past and run into his saloon. He was still undecided when Wheaton spoke without taking his eyes off those moving riders.

"Johnny, I know something about you." Hub turned and looked down. "I know you were egging McElhaney to find that missing three thousand dollars. Now I'm going to tell you something, an' you'd better believe me. There never was three thousand dollars. There was only nine thousand dollars. That's all there ever was."

"But the express company said they'd been robbed. . . ."

"I don't care what they said. That nine thousand dollars wasn't their money. I'm almost positive of that. Likely, at this late date, we'll never recover their twelve thousand anyway. Whoever got that is hundreds of miles away by now."

"You mean . . . Frank Travis really wasn't the robber?"

Hub Wheaton turned at a slight sound. Amy Morgan was there behind him in a white blouse and a buckskin-colored riding skirt. He forgot Fleharty altogether to stare.

"Where is Lew?" Amy asked.

"At the hotel."

"Hubbell, why didn't you tell me, too, what happened this morning?"

"You mean about McElhaney and this Travis feller?" asked Hub. "Well, Amy, Lew asked me not to frighten you with it."

Amy looked exasperated. "Hubbell," she said crisply, "I am the one who was responsible for Parker Travis being out on the stage road this morning. It was I who put him where McElhaney found him. Do you know what he'll think about me for what happened to him out there?"

Hubbell didn't answer this. He frowned a little and said:

"Who told you about McElhaney?"

"Charley did. Right after you and Lew left the ranch this afternoon, Charley came to me with a little note my uncle had left with the cook for him. In the note it said Lew was coming to town with you to see Parker Travis. . . ."

"Yes? What else did it say, Amy?"

"It said for Charley to saddle up and get out of the country at once, for him to write Lew when he settled somewhere, and Lew would send him money."

Behind Sheriff Wheaton, Johnny Fleharty made a little sigh of sound. Hubbell swung angrily on him. "Go on, crawl back in your rat hole, an', if you don't keep that double-hinged tongue of yours quiet, I'll personally carve it out of you an' make a necktie out of it. Beat it!"

Fleharty fled around them into the Great Northern. At the hitch rack out where Amy had tied her animal, several cowboys came up, got down, tied up, and paused to stare admiringly at Amy. Hub Wheaton took her arm and started along southward.

"It's working out all right," he told her. "Lew was smart. I just can't imagine why he didn't want me to know he was sending Charley away, though."

Amy looked up at the shadow of trouble mantling Wheaton's countenance. "Because he wasn't sure you wouldn't want to arrest Charley, Hubbell."

"Why would I arrest him?" Wheaton asked, puzzled.

"For murder," said Amy as she freed her arm and swept on into the hotel lobby.

# X

Parker recognized Lewis Morgan the instant he saw him in the gloomy corridor outside his hotel room. He nodded without speaking and Morgan did the same back again.

Parker unlocked his door, pushed it back, and motioned Morgan in ahead of him. He afterward closed the door, leaned upon it, and put a considering look forward where the owner of Lincoln Ranch halted and turned about.

"All right," said Parker. "Sheriff Wheaton told me you had something to say. Say it."

Morgan removed his hat, tossed it aside, and looked straight at Travis. "I'd like to see that bill of sale Wheaton says you have, before I say anything."

Parker dug the paper out, wordlessly handed it over, and continued to stand by the door, watching Morgan read it. Parker saw the slackness of Morgan's muscles, the grayness of his lips. He stood waiting for Morgan to speak.

Morgan made a little feeble gesture. "What can I say?" he muttered. "I think this is probably true."

"It's true, all right!" exclaimed Parker.

Morgan nodded dumbly. "I wired Arizona the minute I got to town . . . after Hub Wheaton told me what you'd said and what you'd shown him. The answer'll be along soon now."

"What then?" asked Parker dryly. "You going to offer me cash, Mister Morgan?"

"Would cash do it, Travis?"

Parker shook his head.

"No, I didn't think it would."

"Only justice will satisfy me, Mister Morgan."

"You mean . . . with guns?"

Parker shook his head again. "I didn't have that in mind, exactly, although apparently Ace McElhaney did. I had in mind a fair court trial for every man connected with my brother's killing."

Morgan dropped the bill of sale upon the room's only bed. He brought forth a limp handkerchief and mopped perspiration. "All those men weren't involved."

"Yes they were. Every man who rode with you and Sheriff Wheaton's brother the day my brother was killed is involved. I'll accept nothing less than a trial for every one of them."

"Travis, listen to me. McElhaney is dead. Can't you be satisfied with that? What good can a trial do for the others? They didn't even see your brother shot. They weren't even close enough to hear the shots."

"A lot of them aren't even close enough right now to serve a court summons on, Morgan."

Lew looked startled. "What d'you mean by that?" he swiftly demanded, his expression guilty.

Parker didn't make any immediate reply. A black suspicion sprang through him. "I meant," he said slowly, watching Morgan's eyes, "that I sat outside this afternoon and counted nine riders with bedrolls and canteens hit the southward trail out of Laramie." Parker paused, cocked a wry eye, and said: "But you just made me suspect something else, the way you looked when I said that. Tell me, Morgan, where did you tell Charley Swindin, your ranch foreman, to hide out?"

Lew turned, walked to the window, looked out a moment, turned, and walked back. His eyes were suddenly imploring. "Name what you want as an alternative to all this and I'll give it to you, Travis."

"I want Swindin first. After that, I'll see the rest of you tried for being accessories to murder."

"Travis, give us a chance. We know now what we did. Give us a chance to. . . ."

"Yeah," broke in Parker. "I'll give you the same rotten chance you gave my brother." Again Parker cocked his head with that same dry expression. "Of course, you can try to compound it by having me murdered, too, Morgan, like your niece did this morning with McElhaney. But I'll promise you one thing if you try it. You'll be dead, too, if I'm able to draw a breath afterward."

Lew was stunned. "My niece? Are you talking about Amy? She has nothing whatever to do with this."

"One thing at a time," growled Parker. "Where did you send Swindin?"

"Away. You can't blame me for wanting to save a man's life, Travis."

"No, I wouldn't blame you for that, Morgan. That's what Frank was trying to do on that thoroughbred horse I gave him, when your former sheriff and your foreman rode him down and shot him like a rabid dog."

Lew Morgan was breathing hard; this was the only sound in the room for a little while.

Parker said again: "Where is Swindin?"

"I don't know. That's the truth. I told him to get away. To go a long way off. I didn't say where he was to go, only that he was to leave at once . . . today."

Parker stood there dourly considering the cattleman. When next he spoke, his voice had hardened, had turned grim and accusing: "You feel badly about being part of a murder, yet not quite bad enough to see the other murderers tried in court. Morgan, you're scum. You're the kind of a man who says he believes in law and order, but, when it affects you personally, you don't believe in it at all. You're the lowest kind of a hypocrite. I wish you'd go for that gun under your coat."

The door was pushed suddenly inward, striking Parker. He side-stepped at once, dropped his right hand, whirled, and faced what he thought was fresh danger. It was Amy. She looked straight at him, ignored his fighting stance, entered the room, and closed the door.

Her uncle said: "Amy, what are you doing here?"

She had an answer for him: "The same thing you are, but also to explain to Mister Travis I didn't know anything about McElhaney when we talked this morning."

Lew gradually came to appear puzzled. He watched Amy face Travis.

"I don't know how he knew you'd be on that road this morning. I have an idea, but otherwise I want you to believe me. I did not know anything about your fight with McElhaney until late this afternoon. I want you to believe that."

"Why?" asked Parker. "What difference does it make whether I believe that or not?"

Amy went forward several steps; she was now between her uncle and Travis. She turned toward Parker. "So there will be no more senseless killings."

He gazed at her. She stood before him, cool-looking, fresh, and crisp in all that wilting heat. Just gazing upon her forced out some of the bitterness. "Was it just coincidence, ma'am?" he sarcastically asked.

Amy shook her head. "I don't think so. You see Ace McElhaney and our ranch foreman Charley Swindin were close friends. I've been told my uncle warned Swindin against you. I know also that Sheriff Wheaton, when he suspected who you were last night, also warned McElhaney to watch out for you."

"So?"

"It's not hard to understand, Mister Travis. McElhaney was riding to Lincoln Ranch this morning. He evidently intended to discuss the trouble they were in with Charley. On the way to Lincoln Ranch he came upon you. He made the kind of a decision the McElhaneys of this world are capable of making. He saw you and at once thought that, if he could kill you without any witnesses around, he would solve everyone's troubles." Amy lifted her shoulders, and let them fall. "He tried and he failed."

Parker looked past at Lew. Morgan was running this theory through his mind. It made sense to him, Parker could see by Morgan's expression. In fact, it even impressed Parker, but he showed nothing by his expression as he returned his attention to Amy.

"All right," he said to the beautiful girl. "That doesn't really matter any more, though. McElhaney is dead . . . whatever his intentions, he's dead. What I want to know now is where your uncle sent Charley Swindin."

Morgan spoke up. "You're calling me a liar, Travis. I told you I didn't send him anywhere."

"I think you'd lie," Parker shot right back. "Morgan, I think under the right circumstances you'd lie." He smiled with his lips only. "You can take offence if you wish. You've got a gun. Miss Amy, step clear."

Amy shook her head. "Why do you think I got between the pair of you?" she asked.

Parker looked at her, still with his mirthless smile. "You know," he said softly, "you're quite a woman. I knew that when we met this morning. I just didn't know how much of a woman you are." He inclined his head. "All right, I withdraw what I said to your uncle. But neither of you is going out of here until you tell me about Swindin. Where did he come from, who were his friends . . . where would he be most likely to go?"

Amy turned to gaze at Lew. He seemed in an agony of indecision. Finally he said: "Charley's not a coward, Travis, but neither is he a fool. He won't go down to Tularosa where he came from. He'll know you'll find that much out about him. Most of the saloon girls here in town know that much about him. I frankly don't know where he'd go . . . and I'm thankful that I don't."

Parker stood there with his head a little to one side wryly watching Morgan. "I'll find him," he said. "If I can't make much of a start here, I'll ride down to Tularosa. From there, I'll backtrack every camp he's ever made. Somewhere along that trail I'll run across him, Morgan. Maybe you don't know where he's gone, but all your ignorance has bought Swindin is a few more months. I've got a lot of time, I'll find him . . . and for running I'll kill him."

"That," exclaimed Amy forcefully, "is your kind of justice, isn't it? That's what you were talking about this morning. Not genuine justice, as you'd have had me believe, Mister Travis, but jungle justice." Her words burnt him with scorn, with deepest contempt. Her smoky gaze raked over him. She faced her uncle. "Take me out of here. I need fresh air. Take me home, Lew."

Morgan, though, looked for a moment past her at Parker Travis. "Listen," he said, "I can't change anything, not your brother's killing or your going after Swindin. And words are one of the cheapest commodities on earth. But nevertheless I want to say this. I want you to remember it, Travis, for as long as we both live. I'm sick inside about what I helped do to your brother. So is Hub Wheaton. If I could give money or cattle, land or anything else I own, to change things back, I'd give them up right this minute. All of them, every damned thing I own."

Morgan stood still with a little flutter at the nostrils, a hot dryness to his eyes. Then he took an uncertain forward step, caught Amy's arm, and walked past to the door, looking down.

Parker let them leave. He kicked the door closed after them, crossed to the window, saw Morgan's hat upon the bed, looked at it briefly, then looked around for the chair he'd left beside the window, drew it up again, dropped down upon it, pushed both long legs out until his heels were upon the sill, and there he sat.

Fifteen minutes later a gentle knocking brought him around, one hand dropping down. "Come in!" he called, then wearily stood up as Amy Morgan entered his room.

She murmured: "My uncle's hat."

He handed it to her. She looked at him. He was mute.

She passed over to the door, turned, and said—"Mister

Travis, it matters to me whether or not you believe me."—then she was gone and he stood, looking at the blank place where she'd been.

# XI

Two hours later Parker Travis was still sitting at his upstairs window, watching the lamp-lighted town below. Riders came and went, off work for the night and bent on the powerful releases range men need at the end of the day. The last coach departed northward to make its eventual easterly swoop toward Cheyenne.

A knock on the door brought Parker back to the present with a jolt. He stood up, stepped away from backgrounding light, and called: "Come in!"

It was Sheriff Wheaton. He stood a moment, peering ahead beyond the opened door into the room's deep gloom. As though he believed Parker had doused the light for fighting purposes, Hub said: "Stand easy, Travis. I come in peace."

"Then come in and close the door."

Wheaton did this. He said: "You worryin' about another bushwhacker, sittin' in the dark up here?"

"Not exactly." Parker resumed his seat by the window. "Pull up a chair if you wish."

Wheaton did that. As he sank down upon it, he mightily sighed. "Hot tonight. Thirty degrees cooler than daytime, but still damned hot."

Parker sat looking down upon Laramie, saying nothing or looking around at the sheriff.

Wheaton turned loosely where he sat. He, too, ran a solemn look out over his town. Then he suddenly said: "You weren't the only one who lost, Travis."

Parker still said nothing or moved.

"I talked to Amy before she an' Lew left town. I'd like to tell you something. It's personal, and therefore I've never spoken much about it. My brother who was the former sheriff . . . the man your brother shot and killed . . . he was twelve years older than I was. My mother died in an epidemic. My pa was shot to death tooling a stage from here to Cheyenne. But the outlaw who robbed that coach and shot Pa was never found. That happened when I was a kid, Travis. After that, it was just my brother an' me. He left school and went to work for a liveryman. He got three dollars a week and Saturdays off so he could go huntin'. We lived on brush rabbits, sage hens, an occasional antelope, and deer meat. Sometimes in wintertime he'd get a chance to go with freighters to the Tetons. When that happened, he usually came home with plenty of bear meat." Hub stopped speaking for a moment, put his feet upon the windowsill, ruefully wagged his head, and chuckled. "You ever eat antelope and bear meat, Travis? Well, antelope stinks when you're cleanin' it, and, when it's cooked, it tastes like an old billy goat smells. Now bear meat . . . there's something. It's like eatin' rancid hog fat with the entrails left in. When I was real little, I'd bawl like a bay steer, but later, after I was old enough to understand how much Ken was sacrificin' to get those carcasses, I'd choke . . . but I'd eat the stuff."

Parker spoke finally. He looked steadily at Wheaton, saying: "I get the point, Sheriff."

But Hub wasn't ready to stop yet. "Sure you get it," he conceded, "but let me tell you a little more. We didn't have very good clothes, you see . . . oh, sure, the townsfolk helped when they could, but they had kids of their own . . . so when I went to school, the other kids used to pick on me. I reckon I got beat up more'n any kid in our school until I got big enough to do a little beatin' of my own. Now, mind you, Travis, Ken was only eighteen or nineteen at the time, but he was big as a man and tough as catgut. Still, when I'd come home bawlin', he'd refuse to go with me an' waylay those big kids. You know what he told me, Travis? He said . . . 'Hub, you can't lean on folks. You've got to learn to fight back.' It used to make me hate him. I didn't understand why a big tough kid like Ken wouldn't defend his little brother. Then one day he did, but that wasn't with school kids. A drunk cowboy roped me in the roadway and was draggin' me behind his horse. Ken was in the livery barn and saw that." Wheaton chuckled. "He came across the damned road like he'd been shot out of a cannon. He hit that cowboy on the fly, knocked him off his horse, and dang' near beat him to death. I think he would've killed him if some fellers hadn't dragged him off."

"And you learned a lesson there," said Parker quietly. "You learned that he'd always be around if something too big to handle came up."

"Yeah," mused Wheaton. He was quiet for a little time, sitting there in night shadow beside Parker. "Yeah, I learned a lot from Ken. Now he's dead."

"Killed by my brother . . . is that what you mean, Wheaton?"

"Yes."

"And what d'you want to do about it?"

Wheaton did not answer this question. Instead he said: "You know, Travis, when I first knew who you were, I wanted very much to run you down, call you out, and kill you. You weren't responsible for Ken's death, but you were the brother of the man who killed him."

"And now, Wheaton?"

"Nothing. I'm sitting here in the dark with you, feeling no hatred for you, no hatred for your brother. Just sadness that a good man died." Wheaton twisted on his chair. "You told Amy Morgan she couldn't know how you felt. She told me you said that. That's why I came up here tonight. Travis, maybe Amy

147

doesn't know, maybe Lew and Ace and Charley don't know . . . but *I* know how you feel."

The Mexican cigar Parker had been smoking had gone out. He put it aside. "I reckon you do, at that," he murmured to Hub Wheaton. "I've been sittin' here for hours wrestling with myself. It's like trying to swallow something that won't go down. The difference between us is that your brother was older . . . he stood in my shoes, in relation to my brother."

"I know."

Parker folded both hands in his lap. "I'm sorry about your brother, Wheaton."

"I know that, too. You're a fair man, Travis. Would you like to tell me about young Frank?"

"No. No, Frank is dead."

"I took his money from the express office and put it in my jailhouse safe. Any time you want it, it's yours."

"Thanks. But it's not the damned money. That's what got him in the notion to run in the first place. I wish he hadn't had the damned money at all."

"What was he going to do with it?"

"Well, when he left me the last time, he said he thought he'd come up into this country and look around. He'd heard there was good cattle country up in here for sale, cheap."

"He should have left the money with you down in Arizona."

Parker smiled for the first time. "Sure he should have, but Frank was independent. I raised him to be that way. He wanted it with him and I didn't argue about it."

Hub leaned forward, pushed up off the chair, and stood, tall and grave, in the faint light. "You know how I looked at my brother's killing, Travis? I'll tell you . . . your brother shot and killed him when he was doing his legal duty as a sheriff. . . ." Hub paused, saw Parker's face lift toward him, and said: "Wait a minute, hear me out. Ken didn't shoot your brother. He was trying to, yes, but he didn't get it done . . . instead, your brother killed him. As things turned out, Ken was being too hasty and your brother was also being too quick to jump to conclusions. But at first what blinded me was grief . . . and the knowledge that your brother killed Ken when he was legally trying to apprehend him." Once more Hub paused. This time he looked out the window before concluding what he had to say. "I wanted to shoot you, Travis. I wanted to kill anyone connected with the man who shot my brother. I told Lew Morgan that. He argued with me like a Dutch uncle. He said his talkin' the town council into appointin' me to fill out Ken's term as sheriff was based on the belief in me that I wouldn't react like that. Even after we discovered who you were, Lew argued against me on that." Wheaton faced back around. "He was right, of course. I know that now. Your brother died senselessly and so did mine. Do you know what that proves, Travis? It proves that no matter how fair and honest men are, the snap judgments of the best of us aren't worth a damn."

Parker also stood up. He gazed down where people were moving in and out of those puddles of lamplight. "What's your first name, Wheaton?"

"Hub. Why?"

"Hub, you're a pretty good man," said Parker, turning, pushing out his hand. "I'm glad we talked."

They shook, standing together in the dry, hot night.

Wheaton said: "Take a little walk with me. I'd like to show you something."

Parker caught up his hat, crossed to the door, and held it for the sheriff to pass through. Together they descended to the lobby, passed on out into the night, and strolled along without speaking to the first eastward intersection. There, Hub paced along until the last residence had been passed. 100 yards farther along they came to a white picket fence with a high gate. Here,

Hub led out beyond that gate.

They were in a moonlighted cemetery.

"There," said the sheriff. "That's my brother's grave. That other one. . . ."

"I know," said Parker softly. "The first night I was in Laramie I came out here. That's Frank's burial place."

"They don't look much different, do they?"

They didn't, but Parker said nothing. There was, in fact, nothing to say. After a while the sheriff made a cigarette, lit it, and blew out a pale small cloud. Beside him Parker Travis murmured. "That first night . . . I went first to boothill. Frank wasn't there. It took me near an hour an' a box of matches to find that out. Why, Hub, why did they put him here instead of boothill?"

Wheaton shrugged. "He was too young, some said, to be much of an outlaw. That was when everyone thought that's what he was. But even then there were a few who weren't convinced." Hub inhaled; he exhaled. "I'll tell you honestly I didn't want him here . . . not in the same ground with my brother." Hub dropped the smoke, ground it underfoot, and concluded: "You see, Travis, you see how lousy snap judgments are? I'm glad he's here now, and, if he was out at boothill, I'd move him myself now. I'd bring him here."

"It's a hell of a price to pay to learn a little lesson, though, isn't it?"

Hub turned this over in his mind. "I don't figure it was a *little* lesson, Travis. If only you and me an' no one else has learned from this to think first and jump second, then it won't be such a small lesson. That's what Ken would've said."

Parker turned away. He slowly made his way back to the picket gate. There he turned, put a steady look back, and said: "You win, Hub, you win. How about a drink?"

They left that quiet place, strolling along, two large, thoughtful men, stepping on through silvery light saying nothing back and forth, coming closer to the boisterous part of town, and leaving behind for a little while their agony and their memories.

"Which saloon?" asked Parker.

"The Great Northern, I reckon," stated Hub, and made a dour smile. "Johnny Fleharty carries good liquor even if he is a troublesome little weasel."

They turned north moving toward those puddles of lamplight that fell outward across the plank walk, outward into the dusty roadway.

They paused near Fleharty's quivering doors to let two struggling cowboys pass through with a limp one between them, his head lolling, hatless, vacant-eyed, and rag-like.

At sight of Hub's badge, one of the struggling men nervously smiled and said: "We're takin' him on home, Sheriff. Just took on a mite too much o' Fleharty's Taos lightning."

The riders staggered past with their burden. Hub and Parker exchanged a look, and that was when the gunshot came, blowing the night apart with its thunderous *crash,* its whipping lash of violent flame.

Hub Wheaton didn't make a sound; he went down without even a grunt.

Those staggering cowboys dropped their passed-out companion in the roadway beside the hitch rack, threw themselves flat, and wiggled into shadows.

Parker was stunned and did not react for several seconds. Hub lay softly flat at his feet, half on, half off the plank walk. Men squawked out where they were exposed in the roadway, upon the opposite plank walk, their feet beating a loud tattoo as they also fled for cover.

Parker wheeled around, facing southward, the direction of that assassin's shot. There was nothing to be seen down there in the overhanging shadows. He stepped over the sheriff, planted both legs wide, and swung his palmed six-gun. No second shot came; no sound of any kind came from down there.

Men boiled out of the saloon behind him. They piled up with their called questions, their grunts, and their sucked-back profanity at sight of Sheriff Wheaton, lying there in the roiled dust.

A squeaky voice cried out insistently: "Go fetch Doc Spence, someone! Hurry up, too. Here, couple o' you fellers take hold. Let's get him inside."

Parker turned back finally, snarling at those big-eyed men. "Leave him alone. Don't move him until the doctor's seen him an' said it's safe to do that."

"Who done it?" a shocked man asked.

Parker holstered his weapon without answering.

# XII

Whoever fired that shot had struck Hub Wheaton high in the back and near the right side of his body, the side that had been closer to Parker Travis. That was what stuck in Parker's mind as he kept his vigil beside the unconscious lawman in Wheaton's upstairs hotel room.

"He's a lawman," the wispy, dour, and meticulous little old doctor said. "Those are the chances you take."

"No," said Parker, turning from the window to look over where the medical man was working with a basin of pink water beside him. "No. That bullet was meant for me . . . not him."

The doctor peered over his spectacles at this statement. He looked knowing. "In that case," he said, showing no surprise, "your bushwhacker wasn't too good a shot."

"It was pretty dark . . . there were a lot of shadows, a lot of moving men in front of Fleharty's place when he fired." Parker strolled over to stand opposite the doctor, watching him work.

"How bad is it?"

"Bad enough to keep him down for a spell." The doctor, whose name was Albigence Spence, was an old man. When he had come to manhood, guns were called muskets and bullets were called musket balls. He had never bothered to keep abreast of changes like this, so now he said: "Musket balls do strange things, sometimes. Now you take this one. By rights, when it struck Hubbell, it should have gone straight through, because it was flying straight when it hit him. If it'd done that, you see, it'd have exited through his right lung, busted one, maybe two ribs, and gone on."

"Didn't it?"

"No, sir. It got deflected by the gristle underneath Hub's shoulder blade and went skitterin' off on a right angle and busted out five inches below the armpit. It tore through a section of the lung, but a small section, and, what's most unusual, it passed out between two ribs without breaking either of them." Spence straightened up, dipped both hands into the pink water, wiped them, and put a critical gaze downward at his handiwork. "He's hemorrhaging in the lungs . . . you can hear it in his breathing . . . and the shock will keep him unconscious a while longer, but, unless he catches cold . . . damned unlikely this time of year . . . or gets jostled around, he'll probably make it. Anyway, I've done all for him I can do for now." The old man rolled both sleeves down, took up his shapeless coat, and shrugged into it. "I'll look in on him from time to time." He considered Parker. "You going to sit with him?"

"Yes."

"Fine. When he comes around, if he wants water, let him have it. But he's not to move. Not so much as his little finger, you understand?"

"Yes."

"See you later."

Parker drew a chair up, sank down on it, looked at the flushed, slack face of Hub Wheaton, then turned to watch dawn come over the land.

Later, he called downstairs for coffee and resumed his quiet vigil. He wasn't particularly tired but he felt drained by the night's ordeals, bowed down in spirit, troubled in thought, depressed. When the coffee came, he drank two cups of it, felt better, and had a smoke. When restlessness came, he found the sheriff's razor and shaved. Afterward, still restless, he also shaved Hubbell Wheaton. By then that creeping yellow brilliance was coming over the land, the air was turning breathless again, and suddenly Hub reached up, pushing at the blankets over him. But it was an instinctive thing; he was still out of his head.

Parker stripped all but the sheet off Wheaton. He wiped perspiration off him, and, when he seemed especially feverish, he kept wet, cool rags on him.

It was nearly ten o'clock when Lew and Amy Morgan came into the room. Parker looked over where they halted in the doorway. Amy crossed to the bedside and gazed down. Her steely eyes were dark with feeling as she gazed upon Wheaton.

"Have you any idea who did it?" Lew asked.

Parker had an idea, had had it for several hours now. He looked unblinkingly at Lew. "Who told you?" he asked.

Amy, speaking ahead of her uncle, seemed to be probing Parker for what he really thought. "One of the men . . . he heard it in town."

Parker looked down. "It's too bad he's still out. I'm sure he'd like to know you rode in."

"That's not the only reason we came," said Amy, still staring at Travis. "We were coming anyway. To warn you."

"Warn me . . . against what?"

"Charley Swindin."

"Yes," spoke up Lew. "He hasn't gone. At least, I don't believe he has."

"You have him at the ranch still?"

"No. You were right last night. I told Charley to run for it. Only he evidently didn't run far."

"What d'you mean?"

"The thoroughbred horse is gone. So is Charley's saddle and most of his outfit. But he didn't take his bedroll or razor."

Parker, conscious of Amy's stare, muttered: "I see." He looked at the lovely girl, then back to her uncle again. "I had a hunch it was Swindin. Wheaton hasn't been sheriff long enough to make that kind of an enemy. But even if he had . . . that bullet wasn't meant for him . . . it was meant for me." Parker walked to the window, looked downward into the busy roadway, stood that way a while, then twisted to say: "You two stay with Wheaton for a while." He took up his hat and started toward the door. "I'll be back after a while."

Amy said: "Parker. . . ." She had never before used his first name. "Parker . . . let my uncle and some of the townsmen go along."

From the door Parker shook his head. "Swindin's only one man, too," he said, and passed out of the room. He didn't hear Lew say softly: "I'm not so sure of that."

Amy looked quickly at her uncle. "What do you mean?" she demanded.

"Charley has friends. There are those six riders from west of town, for example. They are hard men. They're the kind that likes trouble. Their own trouble or anyone else's trouble."

"Then go with him. Please, Lew."

Morgan's head came slowly around. He put a widening glance at his niece. He said nothing, but he stood there running a brand new idea through his mind. Then he put his hat on firmly and cast a final look at Hub Wheaton.

"You sure you can care for him?" he asked Amy without looking at her.

"Yes, I'm sure."

Morgan frowned downward, but obviously he was not thinking of Wheaton now. "Amy . . . ," he murmured, but did not finish it. They looked long at one another; something came out of her and passed over to him. He barely nodded as he turned and went across the room. At the door, with the knob in one hand, he looked back. "Are you sure?" he asked as though they had discussed what was in his mind. "Plumb sure, Amy?"

"I'm certain, Lew. I was certain after I first met him up in the mountains." Her eyes darkened with this admission, turned misty, and something very close to sadness came out of her in a warm wave. "Please don't let anything happen to him."

"Sure not," muttered Morgan, and left the room.


Outside, the heat was piling up, but there was something different in the air, too, something Johnny Fleharty didn't understand, and therefore didn't like. He wasn't sure what this was, but for one thing Laramie wasn't as noisy as it usually was each early day.

He put the glass aside, fished in the oily water for another glass, and scowled fiercely. Sure it was too early for most men, but this time almost every day, since he'd opened the Great Northern, there'd been four or five town loafers drifting in for ale, a beer, or a slug of raw rye whiskey.

Johnny could think of only one reason why he was being avoided this morning, and that was the one thing he wanted to keep as his own dark secret. He finished the second glass, turned to place it face down upon the backbar, and over his shoulder he saw in the backbar mirror a tall, sun-blackened man move in out of the hurting heat, and Johnny froze like that, not turning around at all until that big man flicked him a look, then walked across to the bar, hooked both elbows there, and waited.

Then Johnny turned. "Ale?" he weakly said.

Parker shook his head, saying nothing and staring.

"Another scorcher," said Johnny, feeling in the bucket for a glass. "Sometimes it rains, though, in midsummer."

Parker's gaze never wavered, neither did he move or speak.

"Too bad about Hub, isn't it?" Parker finally said.

Johnny polished the glass and inspected it very closely. "Sure is," he replied huskily.

"I sat up with him all night."

"How is he?"

"I sat up with him all night . . . thinking."

Johnny stopped polishing the glass. He forced himself to look at Travis.

"Something sort of like a riddle kept bothering me, Fleharty. You see, Lew Morgan told me he'd warned Swindin to leave the country. Now, that was yesterday, so Swindin had lots of time to put fifty miles under his horse. By this morning, on that thoroughbred of my brother's, maybe seventy-five miles."

"He was quite a horse," murmured Johnny. "Not many real blood bays around."

Parker went on again as though Johnny hadn't spoken. "What kept bothering me last night was why Swindin didn't do that, why didn't he leave the Laramie Plains country."

"Didn't he?" asked Johnny, and walked right into Parker's little trap.

"Why, no, he didn't. Instead, he took a shot at me from the darkness last night, missed me, an' downed Hub Wheaton. And, Fleharty, you knew he was going to try that."

The polished glass slipped, struck the floor, and flew into a many slivers. Johnny didn't even look down at it. "Me? I knew it? How did I know it? I haven't seen Charley since. . . ."

"I'll tell you, Fleharty. I just came from the livery barn. Swindin didn't put my brother's thoroughbred up, over there, last night."

"Well, hell, cowboys don't very often. . . ."

"The horse wasn't at any of the hitch racks, either. I know that, because I hand-raised that horse down in Arizona. If he'd been tied anywhere along the road, I'd have noticed him last night when Hub and I were walking up this way. Fleharty, we walked the full length of the road, we saw every animal . . . the thoroughbred wasn't among them."

"That don't mean I knew anything, Mister Travis."

Parker was briefly silent while he and Johnny exchanged a long look. Ultimately he said: "Lew and Amy Morgan are up with Hub. I talked with them before I went out to do a little checkin' around town. They told me Swindin wasn't at Lincoln Ranch, but that he hadn't left the country, either."

"What does that prove?"

"Like I said, I've been doing a little checkin' around. Fleharty, do you know what Swindin did? He knew that blood bay would be recognized by half the men in Laramie. That's why he didn't tie him along the road or leave him over at the barn. He tied him out back of your saloon."

Johnny's jaw muscles quivered. He seemed close to fainting dead away.

"Four different townsmen told me this morning they saw him tied back there."

"Yes, but lots of fellers tie horse back there, Mister Travis. If a feller's ridin' a stud horse and dassn't hitch him where there are other horses. . . ."

"Sure," interrupted Parker quietly. "Sure, but my brother's blood bay isn't a stallion."

"I know that. But I didn't. . . ."

"Let me finish, Fleharty. Two of those four men who saw Swindin and the blood bay saw something else. Would you like me to tell you what that was?"

Johnny was near the absolute limit of his endurance in this. He formed words and moved his lips but no sound came out. "They saw you and Charley Swindin standing in the dark out there, talking."

"That's not true," Johnny whispered.

Parker pushed up off the bar. He said quietly: "You're a damned liar."

Johnny put his hands on the bar top and hung there. He saw death in another man's face; it was aimed at him. He made an animal sound in his throat.

"Fleharty, you're going to tell me where Swindin is."

"I don't know. I peeked out last night after he shot Hub by mistake. His horse was gone an' so was he."

"Where would he go?"

"Hones' to God, I don't know. Maybe he run out. I don't know."

Parker shook his head. "No, Swindin didn't run. He had a much better chance to run yesterday. He didn't do it then. I don't think he's doing it now."

"Mister Travis, as God's my witness. . . ."

"Fleharty, you know why he wouldn't leave the Laramie Plains. You talked to him last night. Now I want you to tell me why he hasn't left the country."

Johnny's knuckles were white upon the bar top. He was terribly afraid, yet he found a sliver of courage. It was born of desperation. He eased one hand off the bar and put it down out of sight where a sawed-off shotgun lay.

Parker's hand dipped and lifted. The cocking mechanism of a six-gun made its sharp, lethal little sound in the hush. Fleharty brought his hidden hand up and placed it beside the other hand again, in plain sight. He stared as though hypnotized at the black gun barrel, at the tightening finger upon the trigger.

"I'll tell you," he whispered. "I'll tell you all of it."

# XIII

Doc Spence was with Hub Wheaton. Lew and Amy Morgan were still there. Two men, who Parker did not know, were standing silently glum and awkward at the bedside, too. The little room seemed crowded. It seemed funereal because none of those people was talking or moving when Parker opened the door, pushed Johnny Fleharty in ahead of him, then closed the door.

Morgan said: "Where were you? I looked. . . ."

"I was in Fleharty's bar," replied Parker. He gave Johnny another shove, harder this time so that Fleharty stumbled onward and kept himself from falling only by nimble footwork.

"I was having a heart-to-heart talk with Mister Fleharty."

Lew's brows drew inward and downward. He looked in a puzzled way from Parker to Johnny and back again. "I don't understand," he murmured.

"You will, Morgan. You will." Parker looked at the other men over by the bed. "Who are they?" he asked.

"One is Mike Pierson, the other one is Les Todhunter. They're members of the town council."

Both councilmen nodded. Parker ignored that. He stood there in the center of the room considering both Pierson and Todhunter. Finally he said: "You need a temporary replacement for Sheriff Wheaton." He made a statement of it.

The two men nodded again, still without speaking.

"I'll take the job without pay," said Parker. "All right?"

The councilmen looked at one another. They looked over at Lew Morgan. But it was Albigence Spence who spoke up. He was peering about over his spectacles, his ancient, rheumy, shrewd old eyes bright and bold. "You could do a heap worse."

He chuckled. "You're always worrying about saving money . . . that ought to make your minds up for you, if nothing else can."

Todhunter cleared his throat. "All right, Mister Travis. You're sheriff of the county until Hub is back on his feet again."

"Then," said Parker, "Mister Fleharty here is my first arrest." Johnny put an anguished look roundabout. His lips lay slackly and his face was gray. He looked at Hub Wheaton and looked swiftly away. Parker put forth a hand, let it lightly lie upon Fleharty's shoulder. "Tell them, Johnny. Tell them what you told me down at your saloon."

Six sets of inquiring eyes swung to bear. Johnny hesitated, and Parker's gentle hold upon his shoulder tightened, tightened until Fleharty squirmed under it.

"Tell them, Johnny."

"Let go," Fleharty gasped. "Please let go."

Parker removed his hand. He was standing behind his prisoner, looming large behind the lesser man. Across the room Amy was staring at Parker. Then Fleharty spoke up.

"It was Charley robbed the express office."

Fleharty paused after saying that. There was a congealed hush broken only by the sharp intake of Lew Morgan's breath.

"He got the twelve thousand dollars. He had it planned so's he wouldn't make a run for it at all. Then Ken Wheaton got up that posse and went racin' out, lookin' for lone horsemen on the plains, and that feller, Frank Travis, took it from there. You all know what happened after that. Young Travis an' Ken got killed, an' everyone figured young Travis was the robber . . . except for that three thousand dollars. Then along come this other Travis, an' everyone got all upset over again. Charley said, if he'd tried, he couldn't have planned it any better'n that."

Amy spoke up: "He said . . . explain what you mean by that. Did Swindin tell *you* that?"

"Yes'm, he told me that."

161

"Then you were in on it?"

Johnny put an imploring look around. "No'm. Not at first, I wasn't. Not until last night. Charley hid the money here in town."

"*Ahhh*," said Lew Morgan, "I'm beginning to understand something now. That's why Charley wouldn't leave the country. He had to get his cache first. Is that it, Fleharty?"

"Yes, sir, that's it. Last night he come to my saloon." Johnny's voice turned bitter and accusing now. "He was riding that damned blood bay horse. Hell, everyone knew that cussed animal. It was a foolish thing he done, an' I told him so. He said it wasn't foolish, said he wanted the fastest horse in the country under him after he killed the other Travis, got his money, and left the country."

"It *was* Swindin who shot Hub?" exclaimed Amy.

Parker nodded over at her from behind Fleharty.

Johnny said: "Yes'm, it was your foreman. I told him it was crazy. I told him to forget Travis and get out of the country while he could."

"That," said Councilman Pierson dryly, "was real solicitous of you, Johnny, wantin' to save a man's life like that. Only you wanted to save the wrong life, didn't you?"

"Listen, Mister Pierson," whined Fleharty, "I was scairt stiff. I didn't want no. . . ."

"Never mind that," growled Lew Morgan, his gaze deadly and his powerful shoulders hunched forward as though to spring. "Why didn't you go find Hub and Travis and warn them?"

"Mister Morgan, I didn't dare. I was scairt an' confused. Charley was out there in the night with his Winchester. I know him, Mister Morgan. He'd as soon shoot me as Travis here, if I tried anything."

From behind him Parker said mildly: "Come on now, Johnny.

Tell it the way it really happened. Tell it the way you told it to me with my cocked gun on you."

Fleharty put out a hand to the back of a chair. He steadied himself this way. "Charley promised me five thousand in gold if I'd help him."

From the bed a weak, unsteady voice said: "How did Charley manage to join my brother's posse so soon after he robbed the express office?"

Every head turned; every person in that room looked down at Hub. He was drilling a hole in Johnny Fleharty with his bitter stare. There was perspiration on his upper lip. Doc Spence put a hand upon Hub saying softly: "Easy now, Hub. No excitement for you. Just listen, boy, just listen."

Parker jabbed a rigid thumb in Fleharty's back. It must have felt like a six-gun barrel because Johnny jumped and gushed words, running them all together.

"He knew Ken would make up a posse. He had his horse tied in back of my saloon just like last night. When the express clerk run out into the roadway hollering that they'd been robbed, Swindin was all set. Just like he figured, Ken called for a posse . . . Charley mounted up and joined it."

Amy was staring hard at Fleharty. She quietly said: "You know where he hid that money, don't you, Mister Fleharty? You told us just now that he had his horse behind your saloon. You indicated that he ran to his horse immediately after the hold-up. He hid that money somewhere in the vicinity of your saloon, didn't he?"

Johnny stepped to the chair he'd been using as a support and oozed down on to it. He bobbed his head up and down at Amy, saying nothing.

"Well," exclaimed Lew harshly, "do you know or don't you know where he hid it?"

"I know, Mister Morgan."

Before anyone else spoke after this revelation, though, Parker said, with a quick, slashing look at Lew and the others: "You're overlooking something, gentlemen. When Charley Swindin ran my brother down, he knew he was going to commit murder. He did that deliberately and cold-bloodedly. He didn't know my brother had nine thousand in gold on him, but he *did* know that, if he killed Frank, the folks hereabouts would be satisfied that my brother was the express office bandit . . . because dead men tell no tales. That was premeditated murder, deliberately thought out and deliberately executed."

When Parker stopped speaking, the room was totally silent. After a while Hub whispered to Doc Spence. The medical man twisted to a chair with Wheaton's clothing on it, caught up the blood-stiff shirt there, unpinned Hub's badge, and took it gravely over and handed it to Parker.

Hub said throatily: "Go get him, Park. He's your second arrest. Get him any way you want to . . . dead or alive."

Parker looked long at Hub before pinning on the nickel star. When he finished doing this, he looked at Hub again. Wheaton made a weak smile and dropped one eyelid. "Dead," he whispered. "Get him dead, Park. There's no one else in this room who understands why Swindin should die as well as you do . . . and as I do."

Doc Spence pursed his lips and made a little sound at Wheaton. "No more talk now," he muttered. "You need rest, boy, and complete silence."

Parker caught Johnny Fleharty by the shoulder, lifted him bodily from his chair, and swung him around as a dog might swing a rat.

"The money!" exclaimed Councilman Todhunter. "Johnny, where did Swindin hide the money?"

"That'll keep," Parker said, speaking ahead of Fleharty. "If he tells you, I'll have half this greedy damned town in the way."

Amy glided out ahead of the others. "In the way of what?" she breathlessly asked, perceiving ahead of the others that Parker had a definite plan in mind. "Parker, what is it?"

"It's Swindin, Amy. He's still in Laramie."

Todhunter, Pierson, and Lew Morgan looked surprised at this. Albigence Spence said dryly: "If that's so, Swindin is a bigger fool than I thought he was."

Lew Morgan agreed with this. It was Amy who struck at the point of Parker's statement. She said simply: "Are you sure of that?"

Parker nodded his head at Johnny Fleharty. "Tell them," he directed. "Tell them what you told me."

Johnny rolled his eyes; they came to rest upon Travis. Johnny looked like a man who had failed himself and could not bring himself to accept this, like a man who was making excuses to himself about himself. His voice was vibrant with self-pity.

"Charley's in town. He's aimin' to lie over until nightfall. He won't risk running for it with Laramie all stirred up over the Wheaton shooting. He told me that. He said, if it was just him, he'd chance it . . . on the thoroughbred horse . . . because there'd be only one other horse around that might be able to catch him, an' he'd like to have it that way. He said he wants one more crack at Travis. But, mainly, he's afraid the weight of that gold bullion will slow him down. In this heat his weight an' the weight of all that gold might make it easy for riders to get him. He's goin' to wait until dark, then ride out."

"And in the meantime . . . ," Amy asked. "Where is he?"

Johnny began to look genuinely worried. "That I don't know. Mister Travis asked me that, too, but I don't know where he is." Johnny looked imploringly at all those closed, grim faces. "I've told you everything. All of it. I'd tell you where he was if I knew."

"Would you?" asked Les Todhunter, looking very doubtful.

"Believe me, I would," Fleharty said with force. "What would I hold out for? I've already told you enough to get me killed. A little more wouldn't make any difference, an', if I knew where Charley was hidin' in town, I'd sure tell you now . . . because, if you don't get him, he'll find out what I've done an' he'll get me."

There was the same ring of truthfulness in this as when Fleharty had said the same thing to Parker Travis in his saloon. Parker believed him; the others read this much in his face. They exchanged glances, looking baffled now more than doubting.

"The bullion," spoke up Parker, "was cached under the rear stoop of Fleharty's saloon. Fleharty told me that and I looked under there before coming up here. It was there, all right, but it's not there now."

Pierson began to scowl. "I thought Fleharty said he knew where the money was!" he exclaimed.

Parker nodded, placing his big paw upon Johnny's shoulder again. "That's exactly right. He knew where it *was*. Not where it now is." He gave Johnny a little tug. The two of them went toward the door. None of the others moved until Parker had the door open. Then Amy stepped away from her uncle, crossed over, and said in reply to Parker's questioning look: "I'll walk over to the jailhouse with you." She closed the door gently, leaving her uncle, the doctor, and the town councilmen behind in Hub Wheaton's room.

Downstairs, in the hotel lobby, people who had obviously been furtively speaking before these three came down among them turned quiet. They watched Parker herd the saloon owner out into the furious morning heat. Afterward, they slipped to the door and watched Amy, Parker, and Johnny Fleharty step out into the roadway, heading toward Sheriff Wheaton's sturdy building with the barred windows.

"That's Travis," said a bearded cowman. "Damned if he ain't

wearin' Hub Wheaton's star."

Another man added to this by saying: "That rumor must have been true. The one about Fleharty being mixed up in Hub's shooting. I heard it early this morning. I was told by a feller, who seen 'em, that Charley Swindin an' Fleharty were talkin' together out behind the saloon last night only a little while before Hub got shot."

The bearded cowman growled malevolently: "I know how to take care of fellers like that an' I don't need no courtroom, either . . . just a sixty-foot lariat and a stout tree limb."

A thoughtful-looking elderly man said: "You try that, Clint, and you'll likely wind up stiffer'n a plank. That Travis's got the look to him of a man who'd be hell on wheels if he got really stirred up."

A woman among the onlookers, watching Fleharty being driven along, made a little sniffing sound. " 'Pears to me," she said acidly, "that Amy Morgan's making a spectacle of herself, walking out there with that man in plain sight and all . . . like a hussy."

All the men turned when Fleharty, Amy, and Parker Travis entered the jailhouse and were lost to them, and gazed in deep silence at the woman who'd said this.

She furiously blushed under their stares. "It's not seemly," she uttered, blustering now, "for a young woman to go tagging after a man like that. It's not lady-like."

That thoughtful-looking elderly man chuckled. "You know, Nettie," he said, "nowadays, if a pretty girl's going to catch her man, she's got to trot a little. It isn't like it used to be. Waitin' can make a girl wind up a spinster."

There were sly smiles over this remark; the men knew Nettie Fellows and her acid tongue. Nettie, at thirty-five, had never been married. She drew herself up, said: *Hump!*"—and flounced back into the hotel lobby.

# XIV

Parker locked Fleharty in a strap-steel cell, closed the intervening door on him, and returned to Wheaton's little stuffy office. There he got a dipper full of water from a bucket, drank deeply, and observed Amy over the dipper's blue rim. She was standing half in shadow over by the sheriff's desk watching Parker, and as before her gaze did not falter under Travis's regard. As Parker was putting aside the dipper, she spoke.

"You know something you didn't mention up in Hubbell's room, don't you, Parker?"

He turned, walked over closer, and stopped to cock his head a little at her, looking critical. "You're smart, Amy. As smart as any man in town. I was impressed with your looks the first time I laid eyes on you. But upstairs at the hotel just now, it dawned on me that you're smart along with it."

"If that's a compliment," retorted Amy without smiling, without lowering her eyes before that critically masculine stare, "I thank you for it. But the tone of voice was wrong. I think it wasn't so much a compliment as an appraisal."

"You're dead right."

"I didn't measure up, did I?"

Parker removed his hat, dropped it upon Hub Wheaton's desk, and carefully put together the words for his reply to that question. "You measured up all right, but not particularly as a woman."

She dropped her eyes now, not uneasy under his stare but so that he would not see that sad and knowing look in their smoky depths. She stood thus for a moment, darkly in thought. Light from the little barred window came into the room, glowing against the coppery darkness of her hair, putting its barred pattern across the fullness of her breasts. She was thinking of him; he knew that much even though her face was averted.

"You've been a smart woman in a man's world too long, Amy," he said, paused, and went on, a faintly rough edge coming to his voice. "Standing as you are now, half in light, half shadowed . . . you're a picture a man could take with him over the years, because this minute you're a full woman, and that's the substance every man's dreams are made of."

"You're telling me to be more woman and less . . . whatever else I am . . . aren't you?"

"Yes."

She raised her eyes to him, showing a tenderness, a good warmth. "I couldn't change, Parker, any more than you could. But for the right man that would be no problem."

"What kind of a right man?"

"The kind you are. Not the kind my uncle is, or those others. You think calmly. You don't do rash things. You didn't ride in here like other men would have . . . with hate like a banner in your eyes and a cocked gun in your fist. You came quietly and you felt your way. You were more interested in truth than in killing."

"You didn't think that before," he said.

"Yes, I did. I've thought that ever since we first talked in the dell. But several times you wavered. I know why you wavered, because you loved your brother so. You don't show things to the world. You keep things inside you. When you wavered, I was cruel to you because I couldn't bear the idea of your abandoning fairness and becoming hair-triggered like the others are."

She had a little stain of color in her face as she faced him, as she saw him as he was, not yet at peace with himself but near to it, his strong, dark face with its tough set to the mouth, handsome, his dead-level eyes deeply thoughtful, his expression more gentle than anything else.

"You see a lot," he murmured. "Maybe you see too much." A shadow appeared in his eyes. "Why should I show the world that it hurts like hell to think of Frank's dying like he did?"

"The world knows anyway, Parker. All people aren't blind. Hub Wheaton for instance . . . he knows how you feel."

"He's the only one, Amy."

"No. I also understand."

She swayed toward him a little, fighting down a powerful impulse to reach forth and touch him. Tenderness and want came out of her deepest thoughts. Yet she held herself away for a reason; he'd need her more later on, when the anguish and the things he'd set as his goal were done with.

"I wish," he softly said, "Frank could have known you. He'd have laughed at you, Amy. It would have taken him a long time to understand that beauty and brains can go together in a woman. Then he'd have loved you."

Her eyes showed a quick break in their dark depths. She recklessly said: "Parker, I want that from only one man."

He watched her, balancing a thought and a decision in his mind. She saw the reflection of this in his face and she breathlessly waited. Then the light faded. He took up his hat, gazed at its dusty crown, and turned the thing in both hands.

"I reckon I'd best go do what's got to be done." He looked at her almost sadly, moved door ward, and said: "Maybe we can talk some more later, Amy."

"I'll be with Lew in Hub's room, Parker."

"I'll walk you over there."

She shook her head at him. There was a wet brightness to her gaze now. "No. You go on. But I'd like to see you when you . . . when it's over."

He nodded a little, put on his hat, and walked out of the jailhouse.

Wagons from out over the Laramie Plains drifted into town for supplies. Occasionally a rider or two also loped in, and generally, although these men had been sent after a badly needed tongue bolt or a new length of hard-twist lariat rope, or perhaps the ranch mail, they tied up before one of the saloons first, entered with the free-swinging stride of willing imbibers, then emerged a few minutes later with the same closed faces, the same wariness, which otherwise gripped the town, for the word of what was in the offing filled Laramie's very air itself. There were two exceptions to this; they entered town from the south. One was a gaunt, battered cowboy; the other was a swarthy, raffish man with a slouched posture in the saddle, but whose quick, sharp eyes belied his general attitude of lazy indifference.

Parker saw these two because they walked their mounts past the jailhouse where he stood. He did not know them, yet a little warning flashed along his nerves as they looked over, then looked on again, too casual and too disinterested.

He did not see another two of the same brand of men amble into town from the north, and another two ride in quietly and separately, one from the glittering west, one from the hot, dry east. Still standing in the shadowed heat under the jailhouse overhang, he watched those first two draw up before Fleharty's Great Northern Saloon, tie up, and pass on inside. He stepped out into the roadway, crossed over, and swung north, heading for Fleharty's place. A man stepped forth from a doorway, looking worried. It was Councilman Pierson.

"Have you found him yet?" Pierson asked, meaning Swindin.

Parker shook his head looking past, up toward Fleharty's place.

"Have you some idea where he might be?"

Parker's gaze came back. He said: "I can tell you where he *isn't*. He's not watching the roadway or he'd have taken a shot at me. I stood in front of the jailhouse, waiting for him to try that."

Pierson's long face grew longer. "I know. I saw that an' stood over here, holding my breath. I've passed the word around."

"What word?" asked Parker, beginning to look annoyed. "Listen, Mister Pierson, I'd just as soon not have a lot of trigger-happy store clerks slipping around town with guns in their hands."

"You can't do this alone, Mister Travis."

Up the road those two men walked out of Fleharty's saloon and stopped on the plank walk, looking right and left. Parker stepped away from Pierson and started onward. Pierson, seeing the look on the larger man's face, seeing also his destination—those two loafing range riders on ahead—said a quick swear word to himself and ducked back into the doorway from which he'd emerged.

Parker's footfalls echoed upon the boardwalk. He saw one of those men ahead speak to the other from the side of his mouth. Both men turned fully and watched Parker approach them. The shorter, darker of these two hooked both thumbs in his shell belt, looking nonchalant. His raw-boned companion, though, was clearly a rough man. He had a high-bridged nose that had been broken at least once and lay bent a little. His eyes were challengingly hard and the color of a wintry dusk. He gave Parker look for look without moving or shifting his glance except to once make a little flickering appraisal of the way Travis wore his gun. There was a reckless slight droop at the outer corners of this man's long mouth.

"You boys looking for Johnny Fleharty?" Parker asked, coming to a halt ten feet away.

"Now we might be, Sheriff," said the gaunt man. "And then again, we might not be. Why, you got a law against it?"

In the face of this antagonism Parker wintrily smiled. Matching the other man's insolent drawl, he said: "Well, now, boys, Fleharty's in jail, and maybe you'd like to visit him there . . . or maybe you wouldn't like that. It's up to you."

The battered man's eyes drew out narrowly. He kept studying Parker as one stray dog studies another. His unkempt swarthy companion said smoothly, with an apologetic little smile: "No call to get hostile, Sheriff. No call at all. We just thought we'd have a drink, is all."

"With Charley Swindin?" asked Parker, keeping a close watch for reaction to this. He got it, not from the tall man who was concentrating on only one thing, taking the measure of this big man wearing the badge, but from the raffish man. His eyes registered abrupt surprise, then turned oily again and slyly deferential. He chuckled, saying: "No, just a little drink for the two of us . . . unless you'd care to join us, Sheriff. Cold beer'd go mighty good on a day like this 'n's promisin' to be."

"No thanks," replied Parker dryly. "But I'll tell you what I'll do." He paused, saw the gaunt man's eyes show dawning curiosity, took a step closer to this man, and said: "I'll escort the pair of you down to see Fleharty at the jailhouse."

Neither of those rough men spoke and their faces settled gradually into skepticism, into suspicion. "You," said the gaunt man very softly, "ain't goin' to escort us nowhere, Mister Tin Badge."

Parker had both these men under his gaze; he had taken that step closer to the gaunt man for a purpose. The swarthy rider was slightly behind his friend; he could not throw down on Parker without first stepping around his companion.

"Care to make a little bet?" Parker asked the gaunt man.

He thought this would trigger action and it did. The gaunt man's right hand blurred in a whipped-back draw. Parker, bracing into this for the past few moments, was faster. When the cowboy's gun was clearing leather, Parker's own weapon made a vicious short arc, struck down meatily, and there was the unmistakable sound of steel grating on bone. The gaunt man gasped; he dropped his weapon and wilted from pain. Parker stepped clear, leveled his weapon upon the raffish rider, and coldly smiled. That man's hand was resting tentatively upon his undrawn six-gun.

"Go ahead," he said. "Draw it."

But the raffish man instead let off a long breath and removed his hand, let it glide downward easily. He shook his head, looking out of wide eyes.

"Help your pardner and let's go," directed Parker.

The injured man called him a hard name. "It's broke!" he exclaimed, holding out one hand with the other hand. "Broke at the gawd-damned wrist."

Parker considered the broken flesh, the blue swelling that was already coming on. "There's a doctor around. He'll set it for you. Move along." But when those two would have stepped down into the roadway, he said: "Stay on the sidewalk. Go south until you're directly across from the jailhouse, then stop."

The raffish man screwed up his face at these orders. "You afraid of something?" he asked.

"Yeah, a bullet in the back. Get along now."

The three of them stepped out southward. No one appeared upon the plank walk as far as they went, but Parker saw from the corner of his eye the faces glued to store windows as they went along.

The gaunt man's broken wrist was losing some of its numbness and the pain was coming on strong by the time they halted across from the jailhouse. He swore helplessly in a singsong manner, a lot of the starch gone out of him. He said to Parker when they were no longer moving. "I owe you something for this. We weren't doing anything. Just come in for a drink and got buffaloed by a damned gun-drunk tin badge. I'll pay you back for this an' a damned sight sooner than you think, too."

Two men drifted out of a northward dog-trot to stand slouched, looking down at Parker and his prisoners. Two more came walking out of a saddle shop across the way. Those four were strangers to Parker; they were cowboys by the looks of them, tough and hard and reckless. It was the still way they stood, all their attention on Parker's prisoners, that made him particularly notice them, that and the fact that those four men suddenly appeared like that, the only men in sight along the roadway. He stepped closer to his captives, putting their bodies between him and those four motionless watchers.

The raffish man made an oily smile. "You're smart," he said. "Smart enough to use us for shields. But, Sheriff . . . how you goin' to get across the road with us? There'll be two on one side of the road an' two on the other side o' the road. Either way, lawman, your back's goin' to be facin' someone."

Out of a nearby doorway stepped several armed men. Councilman Todhunter was in front of them. He moved gingerly up and said: "Go ahead, Travis. We watched it build up against you. We've got shotguns. Go ahead, and, if those four try it, they'll get riddled."

"That answer you?" asked Parker of the raffish men. "Move along, both of you." He touched their backs with his six-gun. "Keep closed up. Make a wrong move and I'll open the thing by killing you." He pushed harder with the gun barrel.

The raffish man made a quick, negative wag with his head, stepped down into roadway dust, and went walking onward with the hurting weight of that fierce overhead summer sun fully on him. At his side the gaunt cowboy plodded along, ignoring everything but the agony each jarring footfall brought him through his shattered arm.

Parker stayed close enough to these two so that no one firing at him, even if he was hit, could escape also hitting one of his prisoners. He had a peculiar, cold feeling between the shoulder blades as he made that crossing, as though venomous eyes were burning a hole in him with their icy determination to kill him.

He was not entirely sure what he had, but he'd thought, when first those two range riders had walked their mounts past the jailhouse, that they were not just ordinary hands, and that they hadn't just happened to ride into Laramie this particular day and this particular time.

Behind him on both sides of the plank walk, as he stepped with his prisoners into the hot shade in front of the jailhouse, men were easing quietly out of stores, armed and silent and solemn-faced. Two of those other cowboys turned abruptly and went toward a saloon. The other two then did the same thing, acting indifferent, acting completely unconcerned.

# XV

Amy wasn't still in Wheaton's office when Parker entered, but Lew Morgan was there. He was taking a riot gun off the wall with his back to the door when Parker entered with his prisoners. Lew turned, looked at the prisoners, finished bringing down the shotgun, then walked across the room.

Who are they?" he asked, indicating the man with the broken wrist and his swarthy companion.

Instead of a direct reply, Parker leaned on the closed door, holstered his weapon, and said: "When Fleharty told me Swindin offered him five thousand dollars for helping, it occurred to me that your foreman would make the same offer elsewhere. That's why I left Wheaton's room with Johnny when I did. It didn't seem likely Swindin could recruit gun hands among Laramie's townsmen, so he'd have to do it among the cowboys. I wanted to be over here where I could see any riders coming into town." Parker jutted his chin at his prisoners. "These two rode past a little while ago. They tied up outside Fleharty's saloon. I wasn't sure about them, but they looked capable of murder for five thousand dollars. Then the dark one there, when

I mentioned your foreman's name, showed by his expression that he knew Swindin, that he and his pardner hadn't just happened into Laramie this morning." Parker looked wryly at Morgan. "I almost made a fatal mistake, though. There are six of them, not two. Just now out in the roadway four more showed up. If it hadn't been for Todhunter, they'd probably have nailed my hide to a wall."

Lew pushed his hat far back, turned, and viewed the sullen prisoners. "I've seen them before. I think they're itinerant cowhands like Ace McElhaney was."

"Well," said Parker, "the tough one there needs a doctor. Would you find him and fetch him down here while I'm watching them?"

"Sure, be glad to."

"And, Mister Morgan . . . leave the shotgun here. Those other four don't know you're in this, too. The shotgun might convince 'em otherwise."

Lew obediently put aside the scatter-gun, stepped around Parker, and walked out of the office.

The raffish cowboy went to the bucket, took a long drink, ignored his partner, and said to Parker: "You got this all wrong, Sheriff. All wrong. We didn't know them four fellers out in the roadway."

Parker shot this man a withering look, motioned the injured man to a chair, watched him obey, then removed his hat, tossed it aside, and said: "The only talk I want out of you, mister, is the place where Swindin is holed up."

"Who is Swindin?" asked his prisoner, looking falsely innocent. "Do you know anyone named Swindin, Buck?"

But the other cowboy, the one addressed as Buck, was too engrossed with his pain to answer this. Instead he sat there looking extremely uncomfortable, saying nothing and getting steadily paler down around the mouth.

"How did Swindin get word to you boys to come help him?" asked Parker.

The raffish man said again: "Who's Swindin?"

"How much did he offer you?"

"What? Sheriff, you're way off on. . . ."

Parker could move extremely fast for a large man. He caught that swarthy man by the shirt front, carrying him violently back until they crashed together into the office wall. Impact made the shorter man's breath burst out of him; his sly, poised expression slipped badly to be replaced by a look of pure astonishment and consternation. He braced himself against the solid weight of Parker Travis.

"Let me tell you something, mister," said Parker in a voice both low and lethal. "This isn't a game we're playing. Swindin killed my brother. I want him for that. You keep on playing games with me and I'll start the killing by breaking your dirty neck!"

From his chair the other cowboy said thinly, "I wish I had use of both my hands, damn you, Travis. Any killin' . . . I'd do." But he made no move to arise, to go to the aid of his friend.

Parker loosened his hold on the dark man. He turned and said to the man with the broken wrist: "You knew me, didn't you? That's a coincidence, isn't it?"

The gaunt man ignored this; his hanging wrist was enormously swollen now and turning purple. Dried blood lay caked where the flesh was lacerated. His eyes were glazed with intense suffering.

Parker swung back to the shorter man. His grip tightened, making breathing difficult. "Talk," he ordered. "Talk or I'll break both your wrists, too!"

The raffish man was gasping. He shifted and writhed, seeking freedom from that powerful grip. It got even tighter and his breathing nearly stopped. His eyes popped; he tried to say something. Parker let go and stepped back. The prisoner rattled along the wall southward, gasping for air and fighting to remain upright.

"Talk damn you!"

"All right. All right, I'll talk. Lemme catch my . . . air."

From the chair the man called Buck looked daggers, but he said nothing. He wasn't certain Travis wouldn't turn on him next, and he wasn't up to absorbing additional punishment. When the swarthy man began to speak, though, he kept glaring over at him. The dark man either ignored this or wasn't conscious of it. He spoke anyway.

"I was in town last night. I was drinkin' in there when Swindin took that shot at you and hit the sheriff by mistake. Johnny said afterward Swindin would give Buck an' me, an' some other fellers we run with, two thousand in gold, each of us, if we'd meet Swindin in town this mornin' and help him kill you . . . then get out of Laramie." The dark man put a thick hand to his gullet, massaging it. He looked over at Buck, saw the fire points in his partner's stare, and said imploringly to him: "It's no use, Buck. At least this way we'll come out with a whole skin. We'll never get the two thousand dollars now anyway. You seen them townsmen come out of their lousy stores with guns. Hell, there must've been fifty of 'em." Those two exchanged a long look at one another, neither of them speaking. Finally the gaunt man dropped his head, scowled at the floor, and spoke through gritted teeth.

"All the same it goes against the grain, turnin' tail like this." The sullen way he spoke these words was equivalent to agreeing with the swarthy man. Then he said: "All right, just get us out of this, Texas. My arm's killin' me."

Parker let them complete this exchange but kept looking at the swarthy cowboy. The dark man read that silence correctly; he also read the compressed lips correctly. He moved off the

wall, went along to a bench, and sank down there. He was beginning to speak when the roadside door opened, Lew Morgan
and Doc Spence walked in, and for a while Parker ignored the
uninjured member of his captive pair.

Old Doc Spence cocked an astringent eye at Parker. "Wherever you are, someone's hurt." He went toward the wounded
cowboy muttering: "It'd pay Laramie to take a collection and
buy you a stage ticket to Idaho maybe . . . or Alaska." He looked
at the broken wrist, reached for it, and its rough-looking owner
pulled it quickly away. "Look here," said the medical man
severely, "if you're that big a coward, you've got no right to
wear that gun."

The injured man gave him a hating look, put his arm out
gingerly, and locked his jaws.

Spence went to work, mumbling under his breath. Lew
Morgan flung perspiration off his chin. As he did this, Parker
told him what the dark man called Texas had said thus far.

Morgan nodded, seemingly unperturbed by this. "Les
Todhunter, Mike Pierson, and some of the townsmen have
already spoken to those other four cowboys."

Parker looked blank. "Spoken to them . . . ?"

"Well, maybe a little more than just spoken to them, Parker.
They brought them all together at Pierson's store, took their
guns away, sent for their horses, gave 'em a choice, then escorted
them out of town."

"What kind of a choice?"

"Well, Todhunter's quite a joker. He offered to let them keep
their guns an' rake the roadway from the north end of town to
the south end, with fifty armed men bossing the job, or mount-
ing up and riding clean out of the country."

Morgan grinned crookedly and started over to the water
bucket. Over his shoulder he said: "Like I told you, Todhunter
has quite a sense of humor."

Parker saw the swarthy prisoner watching him, so he turned toward him. "I guess that breaks up your party. It's just you and your friend, Buck, now."

The dark man glumly nodded. He watched Doc Spence working on his companion for a moment, then said: "Well, hell, you don't really miss two thousand dollars you never had, anyway." He slumped back against the office wall with sweat darkening his shirt.

Lew finished drinking, went over to watch the doctor. Parker remained by the desk and asked the only question he still had no answer to.

"Where were you six men supposed to meet Swindin?"

Texas didn't look away from watching Spence. "Only me 'n' Buck were to meet him. Them friends of ours were supposed to loaf out along the roadway to make certain you nor anyone else got in Swindin's way."

Parker frowned a little. "All I want is the location of Swindin's hiding place. That other stuff will keep."

Now the dark man raised his eyes. There was a long second of total silence; every eye in the room was upon him.

"He's hidin' in Johnny Fleharty's cellar under the saloon."

Lew Morgan got red and his neck swelled. "What!" he bellowed. "Are you telling us Fleharty hid him . . . Fleharty knew where he was all this time?"

"Yes, sir," responded the swarthy cowboy, cringing back against the wall from Morgan's violent wrath. "Yes, sir, he knew. He *had* to know . . . otherwise he couldn't have told me last night where to meet Swindin when we rode into town today."

Morgan swung around, but Parker, already in motion, beat him to the cell-block door by inches. "Hold it," he ordered. "Morgan, calm down."

"Calm down!" raged the wrathful cattleman. "Dammit, Travis, do you realize Fleharty knew all the time where Swindin was? Don't you realize he made fools of all of us, getting even you to believe him up in Hub's room? Why, I believe he was trying to get you killed. By God, that miserable little . . . !"

"He'll talk," said Parker, opening the door behind him. "He'll talk plenty when the time comes, Morgan."

"When the time comes? Dammit, the time's right now!"

"No, it isn't. Fleharty's not going any place. Neither are these other two. We'll get all the facts out of them later. Right now the important thing isn't Fleharty . . . it's Charley Swindin."

Parker turned away to beckon the swarthy man over. Next he said: "Doc, you've set the thing as well as you can for now. You can have another crack at it when some of the swelling's gone down. Now move back." Spence obeyed. Parker jerked his head at the wounded man. "You, too, come over here."

He herded the two men into the room where Sheriff Wheaton's cells were, ignored Johnny Fleharty completely, gave both prisoners an ungentle shove into the same cage, clanged the door closed, locked it, and turned away. Lew Morgan, standing back by the door, was glaring at Fleharty, who was in turn looking in a bewildered way at the massively bandaged hand of Buck, at Buck's dark companion, then to Parker. None of them said a single word.

At the door Parker gave Morgan a little rough push back into the office, barred the cell-block's intervening door, and walked thoughtfully over to hang Hub Wheaton's ring of keys back on its peg.

"Thanks," he said to Doc Spence. "Don't leave town for a while. Maybe you'll have some more business."

Spence closed his black bag, made a sniffing sound, glowered, then strode out of the office.

"You coming along?" Travis asked Morgan, and the cowman vigorously nodded, scooped up the riot gun, and was ready.

"How do you want to work it?" he asked.

"I don't know. I don't even know how you get into Fleharty's cellar."

"I know where the outside door is," retorted Morgan. "I've never been down there, but you can't spend your life in a town no larger than this one is and not notice just about everything around worth noticing."

"What's worth noticing about a cellar door, Morgan?"

"It's easy to see you're not a native of Wyoming, Travis. In a cloudburst, a blizzard, or a Laramie Plains twister, a cellar door can be the difference between surviving and dying."

Parker smiled. "Excuse me. Down in Arizona we welcome cloudbursts and we don't have twisters. Come on, let's get this over with."

They left the sheriff's office for the corrugated heat waves that were moving in gentle waves in the yonder roadway. Walking side-by-side through this writhing heat, Lew Morgan said: "I hope to hell there's no roadside window to that cellar. Swindin'll see us coming if there is."

They'd walked 100 feet when Morgan said this. Parker, squinting ahead through sun blast, was unconcerned. "There isn't," he said. "If there had been, he'd have shot me two hours ago. I gave him every chance then."

# XVI

Fleharty's Great Northern Saloon was an old building; old-timers on the Laramie Plains recalled it as having been a log fort, a trading post, and later a military stockade. There was the barroom, which was long, and two smaller rooms off the barroom, one at each end of the bar itself. Johnny had used the northernmost of these rooms as a combination storeroom and office. The southerly room had a bed and dresser in it; sometimes Fleharty stayed in that room, and, being a bachelor, it was sufficient for his needs.

The cellar beneath the Great Northern had originally been excavated by troopers when the Indian troubles were at their height upon the plains, and several regiments had been billeted at old Fort Laramie. Neither Parker Travis nor Lew Morgan knew the size of that cellar.

When they came to the saloon, they paused outside, looking along the easterly wall. Large old fir logs lay close to the ground here. There was no cement foundation under Fleharty's saloon, or for that matter under any other building in Laramie that had been erected at the same time as the saloon.

After studying this condition for a while, Parker said: "If there's a hole under this building, it was dug long after the saloon was put up."

Morgan said that this was so; he said other cellars under other old structures in Laramie had been dug the same way.

They moved carefully along that east wall. Behind Fleharty's place was a refuse-laden alleyway running north and south, from the upper beginning of town to the southward limits. Morgan touched Parker's arm and pointed over where a slanting, weathered door lay low against the ground.

"That's it," he murmured. "All we have to do is walk over, throw back that door, and. . . ." Morgan looked up sardonically. "All hell will bust loose."

A man appeared up the alley northward. He stepped out, stared, then stepped back beyond sight again. Parker saw the man and looked inquiringly around. Morgan, who had also seen him, said indifferently, his gaze going back to that cellar door: "Mike Pierson. There's bound to be others. In fact, I rather imagine every man who backed you against those four cowboys will be around here somewhere."

Parker nodded. "With guns," he dryly said, also returning his gaze to the door. "Tell me something, Morgan. Just how good is

Swindin with guns?"

"He's good. There are faster men, but he's accurate." Morgan shrugged. "He'll probably have a Winchester down there with him. We can hope he doesn't have a shotgun. If he has, and if he gets a chance to use it, no two men alive could go into the cellar and come out walkin' upright."

Parker started onward. When Morgan came up even, he said: "If that damned door is our only way in, we've got a real problem."

"There's another way down. Inside the saloon behind the bar is a trap door. But it goes down a ladder, I've heard, and you know what that means. The second anyone opens that trap door and pokes his shanks downward, Swindin blows them to kingdom come."

They made a quiet circuit of the saloon and ended up back where they'd originally stood, looking at the door. Morgan wagged his head. "Rush him," he growled. "Rush him or starve him out. That's all I can see to do."

Parker made no comment. He walked over a little closer to the building, leaned on Fleharty's water pump there, and furrowed his brow. Behind him, back where Lew Morgan stood, several townsmen silently drifted up. Parker could hear them speaking in a hushed manner to Lew. The entire atmosphere around Fleharty's saloon was quiet. It reminded him how men acted down in Arizona when they were stalking a rattlesnake den. They tiptoed to avoid alerting the rattlers by footfall reverberations. They spoke in whispers. They looked constantly about them on the ground.

Unexpectedly, out of this very similarity, came the answer to Parker's riddle. Rattlesnakes in Arizona, especially during the fierce summers, had a habit of slithering into towns, into cool garden patches, under houses and sheds and woodpiles, seeking relief from the murderous heat. Arizonans, for generations accepting the summertime invasion of these deadly reptiles, had long since learned the folly of poking around with sticks, of trying patiently to wait out snakes that could slumber for days on end when they had a stomach full of baby birds or mice. Trial and error had long since provided them with a never failing method of getting the snakes out where they could be killed.

This method occurred to Parker now, as he stood there, considering Swindin's dark, cool den under Fleharty's building. He twisted, beckoned to Lew and the townsmen standing back there with him. Morgan and the others walked softly forward.

Lew searched Parker's face. "You've got it, haven't you?" he asked, when he halted beside the pump.

"Maybe. I hope so." Parker ran his gaze over the half dozen heavily armed men behind Morgan. "You fellers mind sweating a little?" he asked. The silent townsmen, understanding none of this, nevertheless shook their heads. One of them, an older man, short and squatty and wearing a miner's flat-heeled boots and suspenders, looked suddenly pleased, as though he'd perceived Parker's attention.

"Dig him out," this man said triumphantly.

Parker shook his head. He considered those solemn, waiting faces. "We'll need more men, though, maybe twenty, thirty more. This won't be hard work with that many. They can spell one another off."

Lew Morgan said: "What won't be hard work?"

Parker laid a big hand upon the handle of Fleharty's pump. He partially lifted that handle and pushed it down. A trickle of well water ran over the spout and fell upon the hard earth. Lew looked at that water; the others also looked at it. Some seemed more mystified than ever, but not Lew Morgan.

"I'll be damned," he croaked, then at once began to scowl. "Like you said, though, it'll take a lot of work."

Parker nodded. To those mystified men he said: "Drown him

out. Push a hose down under that door and flood him out. Pump in relays."

An old man with a long-barreled rifle turned this over in his mind as he stood there calmly chewing a cud of tobacco. He looked at the cellar door, spat, and said: "Mister, that there the cellar's six feet deep an' near twenty feet long. It'll take a heap o' pumpin' to flood it."

Another man agreed with this, but he also said: "How else do we get him out o' there? Danged if I got much stomach for rushin' over there, flingin' that door back, and chargin' down in there."

A third man said: "Are you boys plumb certain Swindin's really down in there?"

Parker nodded at this man. "He's down there, all right. Unless I miss my guess, your express company's twelve thousand dollars in gold is down there with him, too."

"Well," exclaimed a big, hard-eyed bearded man, "what we standin' around here for? Let's go fetch some hoses and get to pumpin'."

"Bring more than one hose," Lew Morgan directed. "As soon as that water starts gushing in there, Swindin'll figure what we're trying to do. He'll plug the hoses if he can, or cut them off. He'll do whatever he can, you can bet money on that."

The short, burly miner spoke up now, warming to the plan. "He's only one man, ain't he? All right, we'll fix a hose to the pump next door, too. There's another pump south o' us behind the general store. Relays o' men workin' each of those pumps, and extra hoses, so as fast as Swindin plugs one hose, we can shove another one into the cellar, and. . . ." The old miner made a gold-toothed, triumphant smile and said no more, but beamed upon his crowding-up companions. Everyone understood. Some of the men started away. Parker called to them to bring back more men. He then turned and looked at Lew Morgan, waiting.

Morgan pursed his lips. He swiped sweat off his face with a shirt sleeve. He lifted his shoulders and let them fall. "It might work. I never saw it done before, but it might work. One thing. Charley's going to be the coolest of the lot of us, down there."

"Yeah, especially when the water gets up around his ears."

"That'll take all night."

"Which is better . . . working all night and being alive in the morning, or trying to rush him down there?"

Morgan sighed, saying: "Yeah." He would have said more but Todhunter and Pierson came swinging up. They asked if what they'd heard about drowning Swindin out was true. Parker said that it was. Mike Pierson made a thin smile.

"It's probably better than my idea to make a dynamite bomb an' blow him out of there."

"It is," Parker stated. "Your town is tinder dry. A bomb would fire the saloon and probably burn your whole town down. I don't think your townsmen would care for that."

Les Todhunter turned as men began arriving with coiled lengths of miners' hose. On the far side of the saloon other men also came up. These were under the vociferous direction of a short, burly miner who flagged peremptorily with his arms and called brisk orders.

A third group of townsmen came along from southward, down the alleyway. These men cut through débris to the pump behind the adjoining building, which was a general store, and set to work laying hose toward Fleharty's saloon and affixing an end to the nearby pump.

Parker, noting the numbers of men coming back from Laramie's front roadway, was agreeably surprised. There were many more willing to work the pumps than there had been out in the roadway with guns when he'd earlier brought those two tough cowboys away from in front of this same saloon.

Lew Morgan, moving aside as men shouldered up to the

pump, read Travis's expression correctly. He smiled and said: "Guns are one thing, drowning out a rat is another."

He and Parker joined Todhunter and Pierson back out of the way. Pierson was scowling. "They're making enough noise to wake the dead. Swindin'll hear 'em sure."

After seeing the work completed at the pumps, the mobs of men standing ready, Parker said: "Pierson, you and Todhunter know which of your men are the best shots. Have them watch that cellar door like hawks. It's going to occur to Swindin that, if he can get a gun barrel poked out of there, he can shoot a pumper or two and discourage the others."

Pierson and Todhunter departed at once to pass this warning along and also to detail riflemen as sentinels. Parker looked around. The only thing now to be done was go forward and push those hoses into the cellar. He twisted, saw Morgan watching him, pointed without speaking to the southward hose, which cautious townsmen had carried within fifty feet of the door, and Lew Morgan moved off without speaking.

Parker made a wide circuit, coming down on the northward crowd of suddenly silent men who had also gone as far with their hose laying as prudence permitted. He picked up the hose end, said—"Pay it out as I go forward."—and moved unerringly toward that innocent-looking, weather-checked door. Across from him Lew Morgan, hatless now, his shock of gray hair nearly white in the burning sun, was also moving up. The third hose had been taken over by Todhunter and Pierson. All around those three rear pumps men stood like stone, guns ready, faces strained, scarcely breathing. The overhead sun was a little off center, making a thin, weak length of shadow along the back wall of Fleharty's saloon. Otherwise, everyone in that rear area was pitilessly exposed, particularly Parker Travis, Lew Morgan, and those two furiously sweating town councilmen.

# XVII

The cellar door lay flush with the rear of Fleharty's saloon. The part that was against the building was slightly raised, which was customary, so that winter snows and springtime rains would not fill the cellar with water.

The door itself was in two halves, both hinged upon the outer edge. Oftentimes in the Laramie Plains country, where winds were powerful enough to level shacks, people placed iron weights or large stones upon these doors, at least during storm seasons. There were no such weights upon Fleharty's cellar doors, for which Parker was very thankful as he got down on hands and knees to crawl the final fifteen feet. Opposite him Morgan was also crawling. On his left Mike Pierson and Les Todhunter were slightly farther away. But they were steadily moving, dragging their hose, too.

Parker got to the door first. He tugged for more slack, pushed his hose up to the very confines of the door, and held it ready. Morgan got up, too, then both of them waited. When Todhunter inched forward the last five feet, his face was white, dappled with perspiration, and his breathing seemed loud. Parker readied his hose for the thrust that would put it under the door and downward into Fleharty's cellar. He did this with one hand; he drew and cocked his six-gun with the other hand. At a nod from Lew Morgan, all three hoses were given a powerful push under the door, line was played out, the hoses were pushed steadily inward and downward, then those sweat-drenched crawlers turned and got away swiftly. It proved an unnecessary thing, this rapid withdrawal; no sound came from behind the doors. No gunshot, no sound of boot steps, no noise of any kind.

Later, when those four hose carriers met over by the northern pump, Todhunter said: "If he's down there, he's sure keeping it a secret."

"And," muttered Morgan, "you can thank your lucky stars for that, too. Otherwise, we'd be taking turns picking lead out of each other's hides."

Parker took no part in this discussion. He looked around, raised his arm, held it briefly poised, then slashed downward with it. Immediately three sets of working crews began furiously to pump large streams of water into the cellar under the Great Northern Saloon.

For a long time the only sound was of metal pump parts rattling, the hissing of air past pump washers, and some time later the sloshing of water upon water under Fleharty's saloon.

Men tired and were replaced. Those curved steel handles never ceased rising and falling, rising and falling. In Parker's eyes this was a bizarre picture, those sweating men working in grim silence. Others staggered into back wall shade to sink down, exhausted from their work. The bitter sunlight burned downward and men by the dozens stood ready at the pumps or knelt with Winchesters at the ready, all focusing their whole attention on those doors where the increasing slosh of water could plainly be heard.

He stood a while considering all this, then he abruptly walked away. Lew Morgan looked after him but said nothing. People were so interested in the unique plan being executed behind the saloon that only a few heeded Parker's route out of the alleyway to the yonder roadway, then on into Fleharty's building from the roadside.

There were men inside, too, at least ten of them. When Parker entered, although he knew none of these men, they seemed to know him. Several nodded and that old tobacco-chewing mossback with the long-barreled rifle was standing at the south end of the bar, skinny old arms hooked around his big-bore musket, placidly chewing and watching with a faded and unwavering set of eyes that backbar trap door.

When Parker strode up, the old man interrupted his vigil long enough to say: "I can hear 'er fillin' up down there. I figured that ground'd be more porous than that."

"You hear anything else?" asked Parker.

"Yup," responded the oldster. "I heard a man cuss a blue streak."

Parker let off a long sigh. The old man turned at this close sound, put an understanding glance upon Travis, and said: "Know exactly how ye feel. I been in situations like this m'self, years back. It's hard on a man thinkin' he's right but bein' unable to make sure. Well, mister, you guessed right enough . . . he's down there, even if he is tryin' to make out like he ain't." The old man spat, considered the trap door, and said in a pensive way: "What's botherin' me is what'll happen when he comes out."

Parker had no chance to reply to this, even if he'd intended to. From behind the building a gunshot sounded, then another explosion, and several more. A townsman stepped into the saloon, saw all those alert faces, and said: "He's down there. He tried pushin' the hoses out. The fellers opened up on him through the door."

"The hoses?" asked Parker.

"Still in place, Mister Travis. Them slugs busted hell out of Fleharty's door. They drove Swindin back." The townsman smiled expansively. "Everything's workin' fine."

At Parker's side the old man said: "That only leaves him one way out, sonny. He knows now he dassn't try it through the cellar door. That leaves this here trap door."

Parker silently agreed with this. He listened to that deepening water for a while, then said: "Old-timer, you and these other men move back. Go over by the front door. That man down there belongs to me, but, if I miss when he comes up out of there, you fellers can have him when he tries runnin' for it."

Everyone who heard this obediently drifted clear of the bar. The old man was the last to shuffle away. For a moment he gazed calculatingly at Parker, then he, too, moved off.

There were no more shots from around back, but Lew Morgan came shouldering inside from the roadway. He stopped when a man detained him by a hand upon his arm. Lew watched Parker, standing alone at the bar's southern ending, his six-gun in one fist, cocked and ready, his body slouched and his gaze downward. Lew called over to him.

"It's filling up faster than we thought. Must be up past his knees by now."

Parker started to swing his head; something beyond sight of Morgan and the others caught his attention, turning him suddenly stiff, poised, and utterly still.

Across the room those watchers stared. The only movement among them was from the old man. He continued rhythmically to work on his pouched cud of tobacco.

The trap door was beginning to rise. It did this with perceptible slowness. For almost a full minute Parker had no view of the hand or shoulder or head that were raising it. Then he did; a man's straining big fingers showed. Afterward the wrist also showed. Then the top of a hat. Parker stood, leaning upon the bar's far curving, his legs and lower body hidden from the vision of that stealthily climbing figure below in the cellar's dark dankness.

There was a breathless silence in the saloon, but, outside, those protesting pumps clattered and men's voices lifted and faded, coming on, then trailing off. Parker tilted his six-gun barrel the slightest bit. He could have shot at the top of that hat, but instead he waited. It was in his mind to let Swindin see and recognize him, to let the ex-foreman of Lincoln Ranch feel some of that terrible finality that men know when they realize there is no way out of a situation but death. His brother had known that feeling; he meant for Swindin also to know it.

The trap door continued to rise. Swindin's forearm was visible. He seemed emboldened, acted as though he thought perhaps no one knew of this other way out of the cellar. His shoulder showed. His other hand appeared, holding a cocked .44. Very slowly, inch by inch, his head came into view, around it his big shoulders all hunched with tightness.

He saw Parker, standing there. For a lengthening second those two men stared at one another, neither breathing, neither blinking. Swindin wrenched violently bringing his gun hand up and around. He fired and above him glass broke into myriad pieces. He fired a second time, still frantically swinging that gun to bear.

Parker's whole attention was forward and downward. He was cold; no excitement was in him, and even that consuming fire for vengeance was blanked out as he methodically began drawing his trigger finger tight. Then, at the very last fraction of a second he did something he'd not intended doing. Just before his gun went off, he deliberately dropped the muzzle slightly. He shot, thumbed back, and shot again. Swindin gave out an explosive grunt, whipped backward from impact, let go of the trap door and the ladder he was standing on, fell into the water below, and, as the door slammed down, he was lost to sight.

Parker stepped forward, heaved the door up again, let it fall beside him, peered downward for a moment, and afterward got up and turned away, walking out around the bar into the barroom's center. He said nothing to any of those dozen men standing statue-like at the doorway. He ejected those two spent casings, plugged in two replacements from his shell belt, holstered the weapon, and shouldered through to the reddening roadway where afternoon sun glare was putting its dying day mellowness over Laramie.

Men drifted from the saloon. They looked but they did not speak. Not even Lew Morgan, one of the last to walk out. Lew was soaked; so were three men with him. Lew told one of them to go around back, tell the men back there to stop pumping. He also said to another man: "Fetch Doc Spence." Then he stood back in the fiery shade under Fleharty's overhang and silently began squeezing water out of his clothing. Ahead of him, leaning on an upright post, Parker Travis stood looking straight out over the Laramie Plains.

Silence came; the grimy men began coming around into Laramie's roadway. Some of them trooped into the saloon to look upon the man lying there with pink water around him. Some showed more interest in the heavy, soaked leather saddlebags lying beside Charley Swindin. Lew had put a man to guarding those gold-filled saddlebags with a rifle, but no one was guarding Charley Swindin. No one had to; he wasn't moving; his eyes were closed, and only the faintest flutter of a sodden shirt front showed that he was even alive.

Parker moved, finally, turned southward, and went tiredly along toward the hotel. Men everywhere ahead had spread the news. As he went along, people showed him admiring faces. He ignored them; he was asking himself the same question over and over again: *Why did I fire low? Why didn't I kill him when he was mine?*

At the hotel he turned in, paused at the bottom of the stairs, looking upward, thinking how Hub would look his reproach at what Parker would tell him—that he hadn't killed Swindin, after all, that he didn't know why he hadn't—he just hadn't.

He climbed those stairs like an old, weary man. Behind him the hotel lobby filled with people gazing after him. At the landing he turned, ran a hand along the banister, and went heavily to the door of Wheaton's room. It opened before he raised his hand. Amy was there, white down around the mouth but darkly liquid in her steady regard of him. She put out a hand, drew him in, and closed the door. She leaned upon it, watching Parker and Hub exchange their masculine stare.

"All over?" asked Hub.

"Yes."

"You got him?"

Parker nodded.

"He's dead?"

"No, not dead."

Hub's eyes puckered a little. They held to Parker's face for a long time without moving. The silence drew out to its maximum limit.

Hub gently nodded. "Yeah," he softly said. "Yeah, Park, I know."

Parker turned, saw Amy watching him, too, and said: "I don't know what made me do it. I held low at the last minute. I put two slugs into him . . . one in each shoulder. I was holding on his eyes before that . . . right between them." He looked and acted disappointed in himself; the memory of his murdered brother reproached him for that poorly done job. All the sustaining drive was gone out of him. There was no sense of triumph, no sense of satisfaction at all. "I wanted to kill him, but I didn't."

"I've been there," murmured Hub. "It's like an invisible hand comes at the last second and pushes the barrel down. Park, let me tell you something. No man ever lived to regret *not* killing another man when he had the chance, but the West's full of men who live constantly with regrets about killing other men. Listen to me. You did just right. You did what a *real* man would've done . . . not a trigger-happy man."

Amy put her hand upon Parker's arm. "Hub's right. Ever since I left you and returned to this room, we've been talking. He's right, Parker. You'll know that's so when you're yourself again." Her fingers tightened on his arm, holding him. "I wanted you to come back. I didn't even care how you got Swindin. I just wanted you back again." Her fingers loosened, fell away; her smoky eyes were tenderly on him. "I was being a woman, thinking like that, a *female* woman, not the cold, logical woman you accused me of being over in Hub's office. I guess it took a certain kind of man to make me become that kind of a woman."

Parker's eyes flickered when the door opened behind him. Lew Morgan strode in, still wet and disheveled. He looked at those solemn faces and had the good sense to keep quiet.

Parker stepped past Lew. He walked out of the room, left the door ajar, and passed on down the hall. Amy straightened up off the wall, turning toward the door.

"Close it," Hub said to Lew. Morgan, not immediately comprehending, did not move until Amy was part way along. Then, with sudden understanding, he caught her, drew her back inside, and pushed at the door.

Hub said: "Amy, let him go. He's got to find the answer."

"Will he come back, Hub?"

"He'll come back. They always come back. Some take longer than others, but they always return. It's not easy . . . after the last gunshot echo has died . . . to live with yourself. But with him it's maybe even harder. He didn't kill when he thought he should have. He's going out by his brother's grave, I think, and ask himself over and over . . . 'Why, why did I fire low?'" Hub paused to breathe shallowly, then he said: "If there's an answer anywhere for him, it'll be out there. Have patience, Amy. He'll come back to you."

Outside, where that lowering hot sun was staining the Laramie Plains blood-red, there was a residual sound of diminishing excitement in town. It rose up to Hub Wheaton's roadside window and for a long while was the only sound in that room.

# ABOUT THE AUTHOR

**Lauran Paine** who, under his own name and various pseudonyms has written over 1,000 books, was born in Duluth, Minnesota. His family moved to California when he was at a young age and his apprenticeship as a Western writer came about through the years he spent in the livestock trade, rodeos, and even motion pictures where he served as an extra because of his expert horsemanship in several films starring movie cowboy Johnny Mack Brown. In the late 1930s, Paine trapped wild horses in northern Arizona and even, for a time, worked as a professional farrier. Paine came to know the Old West through the eyes of many who had been born in the previous century, and he learned that Western life had been very different from the way it was portrayed on the screen. "I knew men who had killed other men," he later recalled. "But they were the exceptions. Prior to and during the Depression, people were just too busy eking out an existence to indulge in Saturday-night brawls." He served in the U.S. Navy in the Second World War and began writing for Western pulp magazines following his discharge. It is interesting to note that all of his earliest novels (written under his own name and the pseudonym Mark Carrel) were published in the British market and he soon had as strong a following in that country as in the United States. Paine's Western fiction is characterized by strong plots, authenticity, an apparently effortless ability to construct situation and character, and a preference for building his stories upon a solid foundation of historical fact. *Adobe Empire* (1956), one of his best novels, is a fictionalized account of the last twenty years in the life of trader William Bent and, in an off-trail way, has a melancholy, bittersweet texture that is not easily forgotten. In later novels like *The White Bird* (Five Star Westerns, 1997) and *Cache Cañon* (Five Star Westerns, 1998), he showed that the special magic and power of his stories and characters had only matured along with his basic themes of changing times, changing attitudes, learning from experience, respecting Nature, and the yearning for a simpler, more moderate way of life. His next Five Star Western will be *Halfmoon Ranch*.